FCH

The
Doomsday Trail

Also available in Large Print
by Ray Hogan:

The Doomsday Bullet
The Glory Trail
Lawman's Choice
Man Without a Gun
The Peace Keeper
Pilgrim
The Proving Gun
The Yesterday Rider
The Vengeance of
   Fortuna West

Ray Hogan

The Doomsday Trail

G.K.HALL&CO.
Boston, Massachusetts
1984

Published in Large Print by arrangement with
Doubleday & Company, Inc.

British Commonwealth rights courtesy of
Scott Meredith Literary Agents, Inc.

G. K. Hall Large Print Series

Set in 16 pt Times Roman

Library of Congress Cataloging in Publication Data

Hogan, Ray, 1908–
  The doomsday trail.

  Published in large print.
  1. Large type books. I. Title.
[PS3358.03473D65 1984]   813'.54   84–15803
ISBN 0–8161–3722–6 (lg. print)

To the men like John Rye who lived, fought, and died to make the West safe for civilization.

One

John Rye, hard-set, unsmiling face in a deep study, drew to a halt at the edge of the shadow-filled brush. The fire, a distant red circle in the night, toward which he had been moving steadily, had abruptly winked out. Careful as he was, the killer had apparently detected his approach and doused the campfire.

The lawman shifted impatiently beneath the woolen poncho he'd dropped over his shoulders as protection against the spring chill. Just over the Wyoming border in Colorado, he was not too far from the towering Rockies, where the snow still lay deep in the canyons and was banked thick around the rugged peaks. He should have remembered how

1

far sound can carry on a cold, clear night.

It had been a blind pursuit, the sort that Rye, often referred to as the Doomsday Marshal because of the ruthless manner in which he went about his profession, was not particularly fond of. Such instances required time, and that was something he was woefully short of; too, there was a dearth of facts, which called for a reliance on hunches and logic and the thinking through of every possibility.

One thing had been in his favor; the killer had ridden out of the Wyoming town of Gellen, after putting three fatal bullets into Judge Orson Brite, and headed south for Colorado on the only route bearing into that direction — the Arapaho Trail. There was little likelihood that he would stray from it. Not only did it parallel the only source of water in the area, a creek with the same name, but it cut a course through steep walled canyons where only rarely was it possible to climb out of the plains above — and that only with great difficulty and considerable danger.

Also, it was believed the killer was in no hurry. He had not only slain Brite,

2

but severely wounded Gellen's town marshal as well. And since the lawman was out of the picture, no posse had been mounted — a fact he doubtless had become aware of quickly and that would most certainly, in the interest of conserving the strength of his horse, influence the speed of his flight.

A few more days' passage, however, and that would change. By then the killer would have reached the crossroad coming from the east and leading to Denver and the numerous booming mining camps and towns scattered throughout the mountains beyond it. John Rye knew he could not afford to let the outlaw reach the crossroad and turn west — which he likely would do; once he buried himself in the broad, wild expanse of the Rockies it could take years to ferret him out.

Rye stood quietly staring off in the direction in which he had last seen the fire, which, he presumed, was that of the killer. A tall, square-shouldered man with dark hair, a mustache, and pale blue, almost colorless eyes set deep below heavy brows, there was a grim sort of intensity to him.

No one knew him well. A loner in the literal sense of the term, he surrounded himself with a wall of remoteness that never opened to admit anyone. Utterly devoted to his calling, he was deemed cold-blooded by some in his dealings with malefactors, but no one ever challenged his integrity and fairness or questioned his efficiency.

His authority as a Special U. S. Marshal, one called upon to handle particularly dangerous criminals and the more difficult cases, had been bestowed upon him by the President himself, so it was said. And because of such, he never lacked for cooperation from local lawmen, as was often the rule where the ordinary U. S. Marshal was concerned, for when John Rye was sent in it was to cope with a situation where all others had failed and that they, frankly, wished to rid themselves of; and there were times, as in this instance, in which the lawman involved had been killed or wounded and it was necessary to immediately replace him.

Rye, fixing his flat gaze on a line of dark bluffs in the near distance, began to probe their irregular silhouettes slowly

4

as he sought to recall the exact area along their length where he had seen the camp-fire. It had been near the lower end of the formation, he finally decided.

But getting anywhere near the spot, if indeed the outlaw had not already pulled stakes and fled into the night, was going to be tricky. The sound of his horse walking had been heard even though he had used care in guiding the big chestnut gelding through the night, keeping him clear of the gravel runs and occasional flinty outcroppings along the trail; and it would take far too much time to leave the animal and proceed on foot.

Rye brushed his flat-crowned hat to the back of his head and gave the matter more thought. Earlier he had noticed an arroyo off to the left. Perhaps it continued to run north and south as did the trail — and would be the answer to his problem.

At once the lawman wheeled, and moving at right angles to the established path, rode slowly through the brush and weeds. Shortly he nodded in satisfaction. The wash, fairly wide, with a floor of loose sand and bordered with rank growth, was there. Veering the chestnut into it, he swung south.

A quarter mile farther on, with the row of bluffs now looming directly to his left, Rye halted again. He was near — he knew he had to be. Motionless, breath controlled, he listened into the darkness for any sounds that would lead him to the outlaw's camp. There was nothing — only the rustling of a small creature scurrying through dry leaves close by and the distant questioning of an owl.

Suddenly the lawman drew to sharp attention. The odor of tobacco smoke riding the faint breeze had reached him. Turning his head slowly, he sought to locate the source, failed. But it had come from somewhere near, probably no more than fifty yards or so away, and in the direction of the bluffs.

Dismounting quickly, Rye carefully removed his spurs, hung them on the horn of his saddle. Then, draping the chestnut's reins over a clump of bitterbrush, he silently drew the sawed-off shotgun from its boot, and cradling the double-barreled weapon in one arm, started off through the shadowy undergrowth.

A man building a camp would place it

near the face of the bluff where he would have protection from the wind, the lawman reasoned; he maintained a direct course for the high, overhanging formation.

Reaching it, he stopped, again tested the breeze for the smell of smoke. It appeared to be coming from farther on — from the lower end of the bluffs. Cautious, walking slowly, silently, shotgun ready, the marshal continued along the base of the formation.

Moving quietly was not too difficult. Over the years soil had eroded from the face of the bluffs and fallen to their base to form an inch or more of sound-deadening cushion, thus making it easy to proceed quietly. However, now and then brush presented a problem, and it required extreme care to move past the clumps that barred the way occasionally.

"I don't hear anything —"

Rye came to an abrupt halt. It was a woman's voice and it had come from immediately ahead — no more than a half-a-dozen strides. He had reached the killer's camp, had all but walked into it, in fact.

If it was the killer . . . Rye frowned

as he considered that. There had been no woman with Brite's murderer when he rode out of Gellen — but, of course, that could mean nothing. She could be the killer's wife, could have been waiting for him down the trail with supplies and in readiness to flee with him.

"That ain't no for-sure sign nobody's out there."

The man's voice was deep, his reply taut. Killer or not, it was evident he feared whomever he'd heard on the trail and was hoping to escape notice. Doubly careful now, John Rye moved quietly toward what was probably a small clearing.

There was no moon, but the stars were out and visibility, while poor, was sufficient to permit his distinguishing first the woman — sitting on a rock in the center of open ground, a blanket gathered about her — and then the man. He was standing rigidly a step or two beyond her near the dead campfire.

Rye let his eyes reach past the couple to the horses at the edge of the clearing. Both were dark bays, or possibly blacks — he could not be certain in the weak light. The killer had been on a bay —

and he'd found no one else on the Trail. Rye's jaw hardened. Such would tend to leave no doubt, all things considered.

Raising his shotgun, the lawman hooked a thumb over the hammer of the right-hand barrel, and stepped into the clearing.

Two

—John Rye was in the town of Scott's Bluff, near the western edge of Nebraska, when the order from his superior came. He was directed to ride on to Gellen, a Wyoming settlement just over the border, and to do so immediately.

Upon arriving there he had gone straight to the town marshal's office, found it occupied by a deputy named Yocum. The marshal, Jubal Hicks, was in a bad way at Doc Whelan's office, the deputy had said, and he'd best get over there mighty quick if he aimed to do any talking to the lawman.

"What's been going on here?" Rye had asked when Yocum trailed him to the door to point out the physician's

10

premises.

"Some jasper up and put three bullets into old Judge Brite. Killed him deader'n a doornail. Shot the marshal, too — real bad — and dang nigh beat Ned Wilkins to death getting away. Sure is a hell of a thing."

Judge Brite — Orson Brite. Rye had given the name consideration as he strode hurriedly down the deserted street in the late afternoon haze. Some, he recalled, termed the jurist a hanging judge and dubbed him "The Neck-stretcher" because of his penchant for handing out gallows sentences.

Rye did not actually know Orson Brite and thus all of the information he had on him was hearsay, but he always took such demeaning titles with a shrug. Like as not every man hanged by the judge, after being found guilty by a jury, deserved his punishment. The way John Rye looked at it, the law was the law and had to be enforced to the letter else the lawless would run wild.

Whelan's place proved to be a fairly large house in which, as was the usual custom within the profession, the doctor maintained living quarters in the rear and offices in the front. When Rye presented himself to the physician, a squat, white-haired man with a ruddy face, he'd been ushered into an adjoining room and led to the bedside of the wounded lawman.

Hicks, somewhere in his late fifties, features drawn and reflecting the pain he was enduring, looked up from his pillow at the marshal. As Whelan retreated he extended a hand.

"Sure glad you got here, Marshal," he said haltingly. "Didn't take you long."

"Was close by," Rye had replied. He was relieved to see that Jubal Hicks wasn't in so critical a condition as the deputy had led him to believe. "You up to talking and telling me what this is all about? Deputy gave me some of it, but not much."

"I'll tell you all I know — got to," Hicks said. "Judge Brite's been killed — murdered. Happened late yesterday. Where was you when the governor got a'hold of you?"

"Nebraska — Scott's Bluff; and it wasn't the governor, was the chief marshal."

"You done some hard riding — and it's good you did. Best you get on the

12

trail of that bastard fast as you can."

"Aim to," Rye had said patiently, "but I'm needing to know who he was, what he looks like and where —"

"Coming to that," Hicks said. "You know Judge Brite?"

"Nope — only heard of him —"

"Well, he wasn't liked much. Wasn't only the outlaws but the regular folks felt that way about him. He was one of them fellows that sort of rubbed you the wrong way even when he was trying to be real friendly. But it was the outlaws that really had it in for him."

"Because he'd hung a lot of their friends, I expect —"

"You're right. He was plenty generous with handing out hangings, not that the ones he hung didn't have it coming — usually."

Usually . . . Rye had taken a moment to consider the lawman's qualification, and then put his attention back on Hicks.

"Was this bird come walking into Brite's office — it's a little building that stands back of the jail where he holds court when he's in town — and told the bailiff, name's Ned Wilkins, that he had important business with the judge.

13

"Ned was busy looking through some papers hunting something the judge wanted at the time, he claims, and he didn't pay no mind to the fellow, just pointed at the door to Brite's office. Couple of minutes later he heard the fellow say something like, *This here settles the score,* and there was gunshots — three of them.

"I was in the jail setting at my desk and heard the shooting. I jumped up and made a run for the door. I wasn't sure where the shots had come from so I just stood there on the landing a bit looking and listening. There wasn't nobody in sight nowhere. Then I heard a racket back at the judge's place and started for it."

Jubal Hicks paused, took a deep breath, and sighed. Beads of sweat had gathered on his forehead and his leathery, lined skin had paled. He appeared to have become much weaker. Rye glanced toward the door as if to summon Whelan. Hicks shook his head.

"Ain't no sense calling him, Marshal. I'm all right. Just need to sort of catch my breath. . . . Anyways, just as I got there this jasper steps out of the judge's

14

office. Tall man. Sort of young-looking. Was wearing a mask and one of them long duster coats that reached clean down to his spurs. Had his hat pulled low so's I couldn't even tell what kind of hair he had.

"I yelled at him to hold up but he had his pistol in his hand and just started shooting right off. I let fly at him with my iron as he moved off, sort of limping —"

"You hit him?"

"No, he had a limp, something wrong with his leg, I reckon. I tried to get off another shot as I went down but I was hurting like hell and I don't think I come anywhere close to him. He got on his horse — was a bay, I think — and rode south out of town."

Rye digested the information slowly. There wasn't much to go on: a tall man with a limp, riding a bay horse and headed south.

"You get a posse mounted?"

Jubal Hicks shook his head wearily. "Nope, just wasn't nobody around willing to light out after him — was all too busy taking care of me and Ned and the judge, I reckon. Do recollect — sort of fuzzy-like — somebody saying it was too late when Yocum mentioned it.

"Had I been on my feet I'd've got some men together quick and took out after him, but you know how folks are when there ain't nobody in charge. They just sort of back off from doing things like that."

John Rye nodded, agreeing with what he said and fully understanding what he meant; lawmen were expected to perform their duties alone and not look to the general public for assistance.

"That bailiff — Wilkins — can he talk?"

"Reckon so, but he can't tell you anything that I ain't already have. He didn't look up when the killer come in, and then after the shooting he seen the same as me — a tall man wearing a mask and a long coat."

"Either one of you got any idea who he was? Has to be somebody with a hell of a grudge."

"I ain't got the slightest idea — and neither has Ned. Probably a relation of some jasper Brite hung — and he's hung a'plenty. I reckon you could get their names at the county courthouse, but the

16

list would be plenty long and I can't see as how it'd help any. Your best bet's to just head south on the Arapaho Trail — that's where you'll find him."

"Could've turned off somewhere along the way —"

Hicks stirred weakly under his light coverlet, shook his head. "Ain't likely — leastwise not till he gets to the Denver crossroad. Trail'll be easy traveling and Arapaho Creek runs right alongside it so's he's got all the water he'll be needing."

There had been motion in the doorway connecting the room to Whelan's office at that moment. Rye glanced up and saw the physician looking on, frowning. It was time to go. The injured lawman had done talking. The marshal indicated his understanding, but there were still a couple of more answers he needed.

"What's the country like?"

"Fine, long as you stay on the Trail. Walls are mighty rough and steep, it being sort of canyon-like all the way. But that ain't the reason why I figure you can run him down — if you'll get started trailing him. He knew he'd cut me down and that I wouldn't be chasing him. And you can bet he plenty quick seen that nobody else set out after him either. My guess is he's just loafing along, taking it easy, thinking he got away with the killing."

Whelan was still in the doorway. Rye got up from the chair on which he had been sitting. "Expect you're right in that — and right too when you say I ought to get moving."

Hicks smiled wanly. "For certain; and I'm sure wishing I could give you more help but I've done the best I could — which is as much as anybody else in town can do, too. Just all happened so danged fast with hardly any fuss that most folks didn't even know something was going on."

"Seems somebody should've heard the gunshots —"

"Probably did — leastwise them that me and the killer swapped out behind the jail — but they wouldn't've thought much about it. There's always somebody practicing down along the creek, shooting at bottles and such."

Rye had nodded. What Jubal Hicks said was true; the sound of a gunshot in most settlements was common as dirt and ordinarily went unnoticed.

"I reckon I've got all I need," he said, "and I oughtn't to have much of a problem if he sticks to this Arapaho Trail like you figure."

"I'm laying odds he will — but that ain't saying I can't be wrong! It'll pay to keep your eyes peeled for tracks at them places where a horse could cut off and head up the side of the canyon. There ain't many, I recollect, but there's a couple or three."

Rye had extended his hand at that point. "I'll do that. . . . You going to be all right, Marshal?"

Hicks took the lawman's fingers into his own and grinned wryly. "Doc figures I will, but the way I feel right now, there's been folks buried that was in better shape than me. . . . Good luck. I'm sure pulling for you to nail that son-ofabitch, and going by what I've heard of you, I reckon you will. It'll be a mighty bad thing if a man can kill a judge for the reason he did, and get away with it."

"That's for sure," John Rye had agreed and, wheeling, added, "Luck to you," and returned to the street. There he had paused briefly to glance about and then retraced his steps to the jail.

Deputy Yocum could add nothing to the information Jubal Hicks had provided; he had been away from the settlement at the time the killing had occurred, thus could only repeat what he had been told. Hicks had said as much but Rye, a thorough man at all times, had to satisfy himself of the fact. And then, fully aware of the need to get on the killer's trail, he had mounted his horse and struck south from the town.

He had continued until late that first night, relying on Jubal Hicks' belief that the murderer would not depart the established route, and made camp finally on the banks of the creek.

He was up and again on the Trail by first light, moving steadily, hopeful of making up as much time as possible. He realized he was actually gambling — assuming the outlaw was ahead of him; the man could have ridden onto the Trail — as he'd been seen to do — for a short time, and then when darkness came, reversed his course and doubled back to take a different direction from Gellen.

But Rye felt it was his best chance — and one he was compelled to take. If it proved to be a wrong guess it would simply be a matter of retracing the miles wasted and starting all over again.

— He rode through the day neither encountering anyone coming nor catching sight of anyone ahead on the Trail. Hicks had been correct when he'd said it was rough country on both sides of the path, which was little more than a track in most places and never large enough to accommodate a buggy or wagon at any time. Nor had there been any breaks in the ragged, steep walls that would permit a rider to leave the Trail. Since the killer had been seen taking it he undoubtedly was still on it, some- where ahead, and it was only a matter of overtaking him.

But when darkness began to close in, Rye felt the first stirring of doubt. By that hour, considering the pace at which he'd kept the chestnut going, he should have some indication of the outlaw's whereabouts unless, of course, and contrary to Jubal Hicks' opinion, the man had ridden hard in an effort to get as far from the scene of the killing as fast as possible.

Too, there was that possibility,

considered earlier that day, that the out-law was not on the Trail, that he had doubled back; or it could be that he actually had, having heard the rap of the chestnut's hoofs and pulling off to the side, hidden, and allowed the rider whom he suspected could be pursuing him to pass, after which he hurried off in the opposite direction.

A half-a-dozen probabilities came to John Rye's mind as he continued along the Trail, and then an hour or so after night had claimed the brushy slopes and the sky above had become a dark canopy, the lawman's spirits rose.

Far ahead in the black stillness a small, red eye had appeared . . . A campfire. Chances were better than good that it belonged to the man he was trailing. Roweling his horse, Rye had hurried on.

Three

"There just ain't no figuring things out sometimes," Red Fontana said in a low, satisfaction-filled voice. "I been looking for the chance to kill that Rye for a long time and here it is, dropped right in my lap."

Standing beside Fontana in the doorway of Gellen's principal saloon, Charlie Durbin swung his attention to the lawman, riding down the street in the direction of the Arapaho Trail. The excitement generated by the shootings the day previous had died off and the town had resumed its normal placidity.

"It's him all right," he said, "John Rye — the old he-coon hisself! I'll bet he's here to hunt down that jasper that filled the judge full of holes."

"Reckon so," Fontana murmured, his small eyes narrowed, and fixed on the lawman. About thirty, thick-shouldered and red-haired, he had been in and out of jails most of his adult life. "He's a mighty welcome sight."

Durbin, a bit older, was a lean, hard-faced man with a full mustache and stubble of beard. He glanced at Red.

"Now, just what the hell's that mean? Rye ain't never nothing but bad news! He's throwed more friends of mine in the jug than I can —"

"You ain't hearing me right, Charlie," Fontana cut in quietly. "I owe that bastard a'plenty — a lot more'n you do. Was him that got Earl hung."

"Your brother?"

"Yeh. Earl was mixed up with a couple other boys in some rustling, over in Kansas. Shot up a rancher doing it. Was Rye that tracked them down, put them in jail. Then the judge hung them."

Charlie nodded. "I savvy what you mean. Well, he ain't done nothing real bad like that to me, but I still ain't got no more use for him than you have."

"I'm finally getting to square things for

Earl," Fontana said, as if not hearing. "Been waiting and watching, and now it's come."

Durbin frowned, clawed at his chin. Some sort of disturbance had broken out inside the saloon, giving rise to shouts and cursing, and over at Fat Fisher's livery stable, a roustabout was singing a doleful ballad as he forked manure into a pile.

"You saying you're going after him?" he asked, incredulous.

Fontana nodded. The lawman was now a small figure retreating into the distance. "Just what I am. Him showing up here is like a present from Sandy Claus."

Charlie Durbin spat into the dust. "Hell, Red, you can't outdraw him —"

"Ain't figuring to try — but was it the only way I could get even with him for Earl, I'd still jump at the chance — I'm wanting him that bad! But him heading south on the Trail's going to make it a cinch — a real easy cinch. And we sure best grab it 'cause we ain't likely to get this lucky again."

"I ain't so sure it's a cinch," Durbin said doubtfully. "Been more'n a few try to get him and wound up with folks throwing dirt in their faces —"

"Because they went at it in the wrong way," Red said. The lawman was now out of sight, having topped out a rise in the land and dropped over the opposite side. "Most of them I heard of tried taking him head on. Was a fool thing to do. Can't nobody I know outgun him. If he ain't faster'n them, he outsmarts them."

"And you got a way figured to do it?" Durbin asked, still skeptical.

"Can take odds on it," Fontana declared decisively. "Way things've shaped up, I can fix that badge-toter's clock once and for good. Like I said, I've been hoping for this ever since Earl got strung up — and now it's come. You can pitch in and help me send Mister Doomsday Marshal to Beulah Land or you can back off — makes no difference to me. I expect I can rustle me up all the hands I want who feel the same as I do about him and that'll jump at the chance to send him to the boneyard."

Charlie Durbin shook his head. "Never said I was against doing it, just wondering how you figure you can do what a'plenty of others ain't been able to. I ain't a bit anxious to get myself filled with lead.''

''You won't,'' Fontana replied intently, warming to the subject. ''He won't be doing nothing — he'll be dead before he knows what's going on.''

''How?'' Durbin persisted. ''I got to know how all this is going to happen.''

''Easy. That killer he's took off after headed down the Arapaho Trail. Means that he's going to be sort of boxed in for a few days — in betwixt the walls of that canyon. Now, was me and you and one other gun — somebody we can bank on like Gabe Malick — to hurry right smart and get in front of him, be waiting —''

''With him already ahead of us in the canyon, how we going to do that?''

''Circle around on that flat, come in below. He ain't going to be moving fast, not with hunting for tracks and keeping his eyes peeled and such.''

Durbin again scrubbed at his jaw. ''Yep, expect we could circle clean around and come in from the east. I recollect there's a place where a man can get down in the canyon at the far end of them bluffs. Take some hard riding to get there soon enough, howsomever."

Fontana smiled, showed his broad teeth. "I knew you'd cotton to the idea. It's something we just can't pass up."

"Maybe so. What'll we do when we get out in front of him?"

"Aim to sort of scatter us out on the slope along the Trail, and wait. When he comes along we pick him off — be like shooting fish in a rain barrel. With three of us cracking down on him from different places, he won't have a chance."

"Ambush him — that's good," Durbin said. "I'd as soon not give him a look at me — just in case something goes wrong."

Red Fontana swore. "Hell, ain't nothing going to go wrong! It'll be a cinch."

"Sure seems like, but a man best not do no counting ahead of time when it comes to John Rye. Man's got eyes like a eagle, and can hear like a fox. We best be all set before he shows up."

"Don't do no fretting about that. We'll be there — waiting. But we ain't got no time to stand around here jawing. Got to get moving. Now, you in this with me

28

or not? I ain't heard you say flat out one way or another."

"Sure I'm going with you," Durbin said. "I got a couple, three scores to settle with Rye and have been hoping for the chance someday. Was holding back only because I had to be sure. I'd kind of like to be around next week."

"You'll be — don't worry about that either."

"What do we do next — have a drink on it?"

"Ain't no time. We get us a bite of trail grub, then mount up and go find Gabe Malick."

"You know for certain where he is? Could lose a lot of time looking for him. Why don't we line up somebody around here?"

"Mostly because old Gabe's honing to put a couple of bullets into Rye, same as us, and he ain't the kind that maybe'll get buck fever when the chance comes to do it. There's a'plenty who'll tell you they'd like to take a shot at Rye but then they get cold feet and back off. Gabe won't do that — and I know where he is. He's hiding out in the hills south of Potterville."

"What's he hiding from?"

"Killed some jasper over a woman, I think it was. Anyways, it's the law that's after him."

"Well, getting him won't be much out of the way, Potterville being where it is."

"Nope," Fontana said, "lose a little time but we can make it up by cutting across the flats to the bluffs, like you said."

"Well, it ain't no shortcut to brag about but if we get started right away, we ought to reach there ahead of him."

Red Fontana nodded. "Then let's get moving," he said grimly. "I aim to change the name of that Arapaho Trail to the Doomsday Trail — 'cause that's what it's going to be for that there Doomsday Marshal."

Four

As Rye stepped from the fringing brush into the open, the woman uttered a startled cry, came upright. The man wheeled, hand darting toward the pistol on his hip.

"Don't — you'll never make it," the lawman warned in a cold voice as he studied the man critically. Tall, mid-twenties, lean build, he was dressed in heavy work pants and shirt, wore thick-soled shoes and a battered, wide-brimmed hat.

"What d'you want?" he asked in a tight voice. In the weak starshine his features looked sharp, clean.

Rye, shotgun still leveled, glanced at the woman. She'd be no more than twenty, he guessed, had light hair and wide-set eyes. With the blanket gathered about her he could determine little else.

The lawman continued to consider her, pondering the possibility of a pistol being held in the hand under the woolen cover. As if reading his mind and wishing to satisfy his suspicions, the woman shifted and the hidden hand came into view.

Rye, features inscrutable, grim set, deliberate manner unyielding, crossed to the man. Reaching out, he lifted the pistol from its holster, thrust it under his own belt and stepped back.

"Who are you?" he demanded.

The tall man shrugged, frowned. "Name's Chase. Ben Chase," he replied and jerked a thumb at the woman. "This here's Patience, my wife. Who're you and what are you wanting?"

The names meant nothing to Rye since that of Brite's killer was unknown and struck no chord in his own recollections. He ignored Chase's question.

"Where're you from?"

Ben Chase came about, moved to the side of his wife. "Up Montana way — if it's any of your damn business."

It was beginning to look, Rye thought,

as if he'd holed the wrong rabbit. Chase appeared to be nothing more than a farmer going somewhere with his wife. Too, the man had displayed no limp when he walked — which could mean nothing, the lawman knew; the killer could have faked the limp at the time of his escape in order to throw off suspicion later on, if it became necessary.

"Headed for where?" he continued in the same relentless voice.

"Texas. Aim to live with relatives there. Now you listen here, mister, I ain't answering another damn —"

"You'll keep answering as long as I've got this scattergun pointed at your belly," Rye cut in sharply.

Chase swallowed noisily, glanced at his wife, and again shrugged. "Yeh, reckon I will. It's only that —"

"Why'd you douse your fire when you heard me coming?"

Ben Chase raised his hands, let them fall to his sides. "Hell, I got a pretty woman, and this country's crawling with outlaws and drifters who'd like to get their lousy hands on her! I plain wasn't taking no chances on drawing your attention — not knowing who —"

"You're wearing a gun. You could protect her."

"Yeh, maybe so, but I ain't much good at using it. We're farming folks — homesteaders — and shooting it out with another man ain't something I've ever done."

Rye lowered the double-barrel slowly. Chase sighed with relief. "Now you going to tell me why you jumped us?"

"Name's Rye," the lawman said. "I'm a U. S. Marshal, tracking a killer —"

"And you figured we — I — was him?" Chase broke in understandingly.

"He rode out on this Trail, and when I spotted your fire I figured it was his."

The woman moved up to the dead coals and, blanket still around her shoulders, began to scrape aside the dirt that had been thrown upon them to smother the flames.

"What's the name of this here killer you're chasing?" Ben asked.

"Don't know," the lawman answered. "Nobody got a look at him — was wearing a mask."

Chase, taking a blackened briar pipe from the pocket of his jacket, knocked the dottle from the bowl by rapping it against the heel of his hand, and then began to tamp shreds of tobacco into it.

"Going to be a mite hard picking him out," he said. "You know what he was wearing — like maybe buckskins or something special like that?"

"Can't tell you that either," Rye said in his quiet, cool way. "He had on a duster that came to his heels. Wore a hat pulled down low."

' Patience had removed the loose dirt from the improvised fire box, was now laying dry twigs and litter on the ashes. Ben, noting her progress, handed her the match with which he intended to light his pipe, watched as she struck it against a rock and then held it to the tinder. When the flames began to rise, Patience threw on a handful of larger sticks and drew herself upright. A shiver passed through her as she pulled the woolen blanket tighter about her slim body.

"The fire feels good," she murmured. "I guess I got chilled, waiting."

Chase made no comment, but squatting, took up a blackened pot and placed it over the flames.

"Coffee'll be ready in a bit," he said, addressing both his wife and Rye, and then centering his glance on the latter, added: "Sure sorry I ain't got nothing stronger, but me and Patience are church folk and we don't hold with hard liquor."

The marshal nodded. He was fairly well convinced that Ben Chase was not the man he was looking for, but had not written him off completely yet. Despite the harmless appearance of the home-steader, the presence of his wife, and the absence of a noticeable limp, one fact remained: he was the only man encoun-tered on the Trail. And assuming the killer had not doubled back —

"Have you had your supper yet, Marshal Rye?"

At the sound of Patience Chase's voice, the lawman came from his deep thought. He glanced at her. She had discarded the blanket now in deference to the fire's warm glow, was looking directly at him.

He could not blame Ben for being careful and protective with her, he had to admit. She was more than attractive, actually a very pretty woman with brown hair wound tight on her head, light eyes well spaced, an ample figure that the old pair of pants and shirt — undoubtedly made-over castoffs of Ben's — could not fully conceal.

"No, hadn't got around to it," Rye said.

"Well, we'll soon fix that," Patience declared. "I made a stew for supper and there was plenty left over. All it needs is heating up."

"Coffee's nigh ready, too," Ben said. "Now, just you make yourself to home, Marshal. Where'd you leave your horse? I'll fetch him."

John Rye was not accustomed to such consideration. Usually persons he met along the way treated him with cool hostility and occasionally, depending on the circumstances, with out-and-out hatred. This was a pleasant change.

"Obliged to you," he said. "You'll find him standing off a ways to your left — in an arroyo."

Chase bobbed, moved hurriedly off into the brush. Patience had brought up a kettle, and after adding more wood to the fire, set it down on the flames. The coffeepot was beginning to rumble and off in the hills to the west a wolf howled forlornly. At the sound the woman glanced up, stared off into the night.

Again she trembled slightly.

"I hate to hear that," she murmured. "It always makes me feel so lost — so alone."

Rye had lapsed again into thoughts of Ben Chase and the possibility that he was, after all, the killer of Judge Brite. That he was wearing homesteader garb meant nothing; he would have had the wisdom to discard the worn hat and the telltale duster at first opportunity. And Patience could have been waiting somewhere along the Arapaho Trail with a change of clothing.

An odd thing occurred to the lawman at that point; neither of the Chases had asked who it was that had been murdered. Generally that was the first question put to him when he halted someone for questioning. Puzzled, but letting the matter ride at least for a time, he brought his attention back to the woman.

"Been listening to them for years, still gets under my hide a bit. . . . Whereabouts in Montana did you folks do your homesteading?"

"On the Yellowstone River," Patience began, and hesitated as Ben came into the clearing leading Rye's gelding.

"Horse of yours sure is beat," Chase stated, wagging his head. "You must've come a far piece today."

"Did, at that," Rye admitted, stepping up to the homesteader and taking the chestnut's lines. "Where on the Yellowstone River was your place?" he continued to Patience.

"Little town called White Springs was the nearest town. Doubt if you ever heard of it."

"Matter of fact I've been there," Rye said.

Ben Chase registered surprise and then grinned knowingly. "Sure, being a marshal I reckon you've been just about everywhere in the country."

"Just about — if it's west of the Missouri," the lawman said, and led his horse to where the Chases' two animals were grazing just beyond the clearing.

"You never told us who it was that fellow you're hunting killed," Ben said as Rye returned to the camp. The homesteader was hunched by the fire pouring himself a cup of coffee.

Rye grinned tightly. He reckoned he did have the wrong man after all. "Name was Brite. Was a judge up in Wyoming."

"Judge, eh. Where in Wyoming did it happen — if that's where the killing took place."

"Town called Gellen. Pretty close to the Nebraska line."

Ben nodded slowly, set his coffee aside, and poured one for the lawman. Handing it up to Rye, he shook his head.

"Don't recollect the place. Now, Cheyenne I come through it a couple of times. Gellen must be off the main road."

"It is," the marshal said. "Man that shot up the judge, beat up another fellow — the court bailiff I think it was — and near killed the town marshal, too. Chance he may die. After doing all that he headed down this way — on this Trail."

Ben was studying the contents of his cup thoughtfully. "And this being the only trail through here you just naturally figured it was me. Well, something just come to me — something that maybe'll help."

Rye sipped at the hot coffee, considered the homesteader narrowly. "What is it?"

"Early this morning I think it was —
or maybe it was about halfway to noon,
I heard a rider going south."

The marshall came to full attention.

"You thinking it could've been your
killer?" Ben asked, sloshing his coffee
about in its cup.

Rye nodded. "No way of knowing for
sure but it most likely was. Time
would've been about right. He sound like
he was in a hurry?"

Chase gave that thought, watched
Patience absently as she spooned out a
generous portion of savory stew onto a
granite plate for the lawman.

"No, near as I recollect he was just
sort of trotting along — like he was going
for a Sunday ride."

Odds were it had been the killer, Rye
thought, and as was the general opinion,
he was in no hurry, confident that he had
gotten away with the murder since he had
seen no posse following.

"Here's some supper," Patience said
quietly, thrusting the well-filled plate
into his hands. "There's plenty more if
you want it."

Rye's lips parted into as near a smile
as was customary. "Expect this will be

more than enough. It certainly smells good."

Patience returned his smile, and as he dropped to squat on his heels near the fire and began to eat, she refilled his cup with coffee and placed it on the ground beside him.

The lawman ate slowly, enjoying the mixture of meat and vegetables, and the warmed-over biscuits filled with honey. It was the best meal he'd had since leaving Scott's Bluff — the only one of consequence, in fact, and it brought a sense of relief and a lessening of the tension within him.

"If you folks don't mind, I'll stay the night with you," he said after a time. "Horse of mine's pretty well beat, and the man I'm after seems to be in no hurry. Pretty sure he'll stop for the night so I won't be losing any ground."

Patience Chase glanced at Ben. The tall man shrugged, said, "You're more'n welcome, of course. Fact is, we'll be glad to have you. We're still a mite jumpy about the outlaws running loose around here, and with a U. S. Marshal camping with us, we'll sleep easier."

Rye had cleaned his plate and, setting

it aside, turned to Patience. "Was a fine supper — thank you."

"Glad you enjoyed it," she replied, "and like Ben said, we'll be pleased to have you stay."

"I'll be leaving early — first light. Wanted to do my thanking now."

"I'll be up," Patience said. "Your breakfast will be ready and I'll put a bit of lunch together for you —"

Rye, frowning, got to his feet. "Now, I don't want to put you to any trouble —"

"No trouble. We get up early anyway and fixing for one more won't make the least difference."

Rye again thanked the woman, smiled tightly, and crossed the clearing to where his horse stood. Leading the animal down to the nearby creek, he allowed it to water, then returned to where the Chase horses were picketed. Removing his gear, the lawman staked the chestnut gelding alongside and, taking his blanket roll and saddlebags, retraced his steps to the center of the clearing.

Ben and Patience abruptly ceased talking as he stepped into the ring of firelight, apparently having been engaged in a family disagreement of some sort. Rye gave no indication that he had noticed, simply chose a spot beyond the reach of the glare at the edge of the surrounding brush and dropped his gear.

— Perhaps he should not have imposed himself upon the Chases, he thought as he opened one of his saddlebags and procured two dark, slim stogies from the supply he carried. But he could not see that he was inconveniencing the couple to any degree — in fact he had noticed relief on Patience's face when he'd made the announcement. Regardless, it was the best thing to do, and if Ben Chase didn't particularly like the idea he was sorry; the chestnut needed a good night's rest for he was in for a hard, fast run that coming day.

The Chases had drawn apart when he moved back to the fire, Patience engaged in clearing up after the evening meal while Ben sat motionless staring off into the dark night. Rye settled down beside the homesteader and offered him one of the cigars. Chase accepted it willingly, showing his appreciation with a broad smile.

"Been a spell since I enjoyed one of these," he said, plucking a burning brand from the fire and holding it for the lawman to light his from. When Rye had the stogie going, he lit his own, threw the brand back into the fire, and exhaled a blue cloud into the cool, night air.

"Sure am obliged, Marshal. This is a mighty nice treat."

Rye nodded, agreeing absently. He could use some sleep, he was realizing. He'd had but a few hours after leaving Scott's Bluff, and that dozing in the saddle. Best he be turning in shortly; he would need to be as fresh and rested as the gelding when they moved out in the morning.

"Been thinking — I've heard of you before," Ben said. "Don't recollect just where but the name Rye, and you being a lawman — a marshal in fact — sort of jabs at my mind. Ain't you the one they call the Doomsday Marshal?"

Rye shrugged. He was not particularly fond of his grim nickname, but it did serve its purpose where outlaws were concerned, he supposed.

"I've been called that," he said noncommittally.

Patience had finished with her after-supper chores, was now sitting on a roll of bedding near Ben. She glanced up at her husband's remarks.

Chase grinned at her, removed the cigar from his mouth. "Reckon we ought to feel right proud having the Doomsday Marshal spending the night with us!" he said.

She smiled. "I think we should feel lucky," she corrected.

"That, too," Chase agreed. "Sure ain't no jasper going to bother us now for certain!"

Rye considered Ben's words in silence. He had detected no irony in the homesteader's tone, guessed the man was sincere, but praise, indirect or otherwise, was lost on him. Being a lawman was only a way of life, often tedious and most always dangerous.

"My being here's no guarantee of any kind," he said. "Never heard of a bullet that knew one man from another."

"Reckon that's true," Ben said. Then, after a pause, "Been wondering about that killer you're chasing. How you going to catch him when you don't even know his name or much of what he looks like?"

46

"Makes it tough," Rye said, "but it'll work out. My best bet's to overtake him while he's on this Trail — before he can turn off, but if that doesn't work out and I lose him, then I'll just have to start digging."

"There's a lot of empty country around here."

"Know that. It'll mean backtracking, hunting for where he cut off the Trail and trying to find out which direction he took. Once that's done I follow, asking questions of everybody I run into. Takes time and plenty of patience, but sooner or later I run him down."

"Hard way to make a living," Ben said, knocking the ash off his cigar.

Rye stirred, changed his position, stretched his legs out full length before him. "Yes, suppose it is. Never have given that side of it much thought."

"And it's very dangerous, too, isn't it?" Patience asked, breaking her silence.

The lawman's shoulders moved indifferently. "Not much a man can do that's not dangerous — and you get to where you accept it, if you wear a badge. I don't mean you let yourself get used to it —

47

that'd be a sure way to get yourself killed — you just take it as part of the job."

"Can see what you're driving at," Ben Chase said. "You mind me asking something?"

"Guess not."

"Why do folks call you the Doomsday Marshal?"

Rye felt a twinge of impatience. He'd heard the answer to that question many times in the past — that he was a cold-blooded killer himself who never gave an outlaw a chance, that he was ruthless, that it never mattered to him whether he brought in his prisoner dead or alive, just so that he did — that he lived high on the hog from the fat rewards he earned tracking down criminals, and so on.

All were lies and exaggerations, of course. Maybe he was a bit on the coldhearted side when it came to the killers he was sent to bring to justice; but he believed deeply in the law and its invincibility. And if he was what many claimed him to be — so be it. As far as he was concerned he was simply doing his job, and doing it well.

"Something you'd best ask the ones

that say it," he replied a bit stiffly, and flipping the butt of his stogie into the fire, he got to his feet. "I'll be asking you to excuse me," he said, nodding to Patience, "but I better be turning in. Expect tomorrow'll be a long day. Good night to both of you."

Patience smiled, her lips shaping a reply. Ben, rising also, said, "G'night, Marshal. Reckon I'll crawl into my blankets, too."

Rye dropped back to where he'd left his bedroll and, shaking it out, prepared to wrap it about his lank body. On the far side of the fire he could see Chase following a like procedure. Apparently, on the Trail, the Chases slept alone. Gun belt off and pistol handy nearby, as was the shotgun, the lawman made himself comfortable, sighing gratefully as he relaxed. After a bit he glanced at Patience. She was still sitting beside the fire. Beyond her Ben had begun to snore quietly.

Patience reached for a handful of dry sticks and tossed them into the flame. For some reason, and weary as she was, she was far from being sleepy. Both Ben and the marshal — John Rye, she recalled he had said his full name was — had dropped off almost as soon as they'd stretched out in their blankets.

Rising, she turned, stood with her back to the fire staring off into the dark night — one relieved only by weak starshine. The wolf was howling again, this time his chilling complaint evoking replies from others of his like elsewhere in the hills. The sounds caused her to shudder, as before.

There was something about John Rye that brought a slight chill to her, too, she realized as she recalled her first look at him — that moment when he'd stepped suddenly from the brush and confronted them. His features had been dark, grim set, and because he wore that wool poncho and that flat-crowned hat tipped forward over his eyes, he looked to be some sort of dark and fierce avenging angel.

And that, she supposed, was exactly what he was — an avenging angel of the law. No wonder folks had hung that ugly nickname — the Doomsday Marshal — on him. He gave you that impression when you came up against him and got a glimpse of his hard-lined face and deep-set gray eyes; at least, she thought they were gray.

They could be blue. She'd know in the morning when the light was stronger. She'd get a better look at the rest of him, too — something that somehow had grown important to her. Just why the man, being who and what he was, fascinated her so, Patience was unable to understand.

Five

Gabe Malick brushed at the ragged stubble on his jaw and bobbed his bullet-shaped head approvingly when Red Fontana finished setting forth his plan for killing John Rye. A large, powerful man a few years Red's junior, he had a reputation for not only being fast with a gun but for physical strength as well.

"Damn right I'm with you!" he boomed in a deep, gravelly voice. "Ain't nothing that'd suit me better."

"What'd he do to you?" Durbin asked.

They were sitting at a makeshift table in an old miner's cabin deep in the hills, that Malick had taken possession of, passing the bottle of whiskey that Fontana had thoughtfully provided. It was the afternoon of the next day following the one when John Rye had ridden south out of Gellen for the Arapaho Trail.

"He ain't never done nothing special to me mostly because he ain't never caught me," Malick said.

"That'd be on account of he ain't ever took out after you," Durbin observed dryly.

Gabe's dark eyes flickered briefly with anger, and then he shrugged. "Nope, it's that I've been smart enough to keep him off my tail."

"Maybe," Fontana said, coming into the slightly edged conversation between the two men, "but that ain't nothing here now. Point is I got a scheme to get shed of John Rye once and for good — if we do it right."

"I said I was willing," Malick protested. "Always did have a hankering to have it out with that tin star, and this here way you're talking about'll be as good as any. All I'm asking for is a chance to draw down —"

"You ain't getting it," Fontana cut in bluntly. "I know you're mighty fast with that iron you're wearing, maybe faster'n

53

any man I know — but it don't count for shucks in what I've got in mind for Rye. You savvy this, Gabe, I ain't wanting no heroes along with me in this! Somebody trying to do it on his own'll blow my plan to hell — and maybe get us all killed. It's got to be done my way."

"All right, all right, dammit!" Malick shouted irritably, taking a swig from the bottle.

"That mean you're agreeing to me calling the shots all the way?"

"If that's what you're wanting — yes! Maybe you'd like for me to give you a paper with some writing on it, saying so."

Fontana shrugged. "Nope, I'm just wanting to be sure we understand each other."

He was wishing now he'd thought of someone other than Gabe Malick to bring in on the deal. It had been quite a time since he'd been around the man and he'd forgotten how almighty proud Gabe was about being told what to do and what not to do — but it was too late to make any changes now. Regardless, when it all boiled down, Gabe Malick would be a good man to have siding him.

"We best be leaving right away," Fontana said then, pushing back from the table and coming to his feet. "Got a far piece to go."

Charlie Durbin followed Red's example, and both stood silently waiting while Malick drained the bottle of whiskey, and rose.

"Was about to ask you if you'd changed your mind," Fontana said caustically.

Gabe laughed, wiped his mouth with the back of a freckled fist. "I'm coming — just that I ain't had no liquor or women for quite a spell," he said. "Now, if you'd just brung along a gal from that saloon —"

"You'd best forget about drinking and womaning until we get this here job done," Fontana said, and moved off toward the horses.

By sundown they were well south of Potterville and a distance east of the Arapaho Trail. They had ridden steadily and the horses were showing it, but Fontana was not of a mind to let up — at least not for a time.

"When do you figure we ought to start cutting west?" he asked, finally turning to Durbin. "Ain't going to be long till it's too dark to tell much about anything."

Durbin studied the low, rolling landscape with its gullies and brushy pockets with a speculative eye.

"I reckon we're just about opposite them bluffs right now," he said. "Can tell more about it when we get to that hill down there a ways."

Fontana grunted, raked his weary horse with spurs and swung off the trail they had been following.

An hour later with the horses now all sucking hard for wind, their flanks heaving from the continuous fast pace, Red Fontana again called a halt.

"Can see we're getting close now," he said, coming off the saddle. "We'll hold up here for a spell, rest the horses, then move on."

Malick, dismounting also, glanced about, yawned, and rubbed at the back of his neck. "Can't savvy why you're in such a all-fired hurry to get there," he said. "Seems to me —"

"You'd know why if you'd use that head of your'n for something besides a hat-rack!" Fontana snapped, again

56

experiencing a stab of regret for having chosen Gabe as a partner. "It's going to be a hell of a tough job climbing down off this mesa and getting to that trail.

"And we've got to do it way ahead of Rye so's we'll have time to take a ride up the canyon and see where he is. Once we've got him spotted we can drop back and set up the ambush."

"Going to have to pick a place that ain't very close," Charlie Durbin warned. "We got to be sure he don't hear us poking around in the brush — or maybe see us."

"That's why we're getting down there early," Fontana said.

Descending from the high plain into the rugged walled canyon through which John Rye was known to be traveling was every bit as difficult as Fontana had predicted. But, by leading the horses and moving with extreme care they accomplished it with only minor incidents that resulted, fortunately, in no serious injuries to either men or animals.

Their good luck continued. Almost immediately after they reached the foot of the slope and were on the Trail, they saw the glow of a campfire a mile or so back up the canyon.

"You reckon that's him?" Durbin wondered.

Red shook his head. "Maybe — but I sure can't figure him building up a fire like that."

"A mite foolish, all right," Malick said. "It's like he was wanting the whole dang country to know where he's camping — if it's him."

"Reckon we just better have a look, see if it is," Fontana said. "And it could be 'cause there ain't many pilgrims using this trail nowadays."

Swinging their horses about, with Red in the lead, carefully picking a route, the outlaws worked in closer to the campfire. Some fifty yards or less short Red raised a hand and brought the party to a stop.

"Pilgrims," he said, staring into the night. "Can see three horses — and there's a woman."

"What about him — the marshal?" Durbin asked.

"Two men for sure — but I can't get a clear look at them. They're both sprawled out on the other side of the fire. Rye could be one of them."

"Sure wish't I had a spyglass," Malick said. He had pulled off to one side, was now standing a bit above Red and Durbin, on a large boulder. "Could tell then for certain if it was him. Could get a better look at that gal, too. Sure don't look half bad from here —"

"Get down off there," Fontana ordered in a low, angry voice. "Reared up there like that they're liable to see you — and that'd upset the whole shebang."

Durbin watched Gabe Malick slide from the crest of the boulder, his features taut and filled with resentment. Turning then to Fontana, he said: "Prob'ly some jasper and his wife passing through, and run into another pilgrim."

"Could be," Red agreed, ignoring the sulking Malick, "and it might be the marshal, too. Could've seen their camp and's aiming to spend the night with them."

"He ain't holding up on chasing that killer — not him," Durbin said skeptically. "He's more likely to keep on riding."

"Probably been in the saddle since first light. Horse'll be tired, too. And he'll be figuring that the killer'll quit for the night — which he'll sure'n hell have to do if he's been on the move ever since he rode out of Gellen. Now I —"

"What the hell!" Malick broke in impatiently. "You two are standing there gabbling like a couple of old turkey hens! Why don't we just go busting down there, shooting all the way, and settle it? If it ain't Rye, it won't make no difference. Nobody'll miss a couple of pilgrims."

"Be the worst damn thing we could do," Fontana said disgustedly. "First off, a man'd be a fool to brace Rye in the dark — and then, if it wasn't him, all them gunshots would tip him off that somebody was on ahead and put him on his guard."

"Then what —"

"We're going to climb up there in them rocks," Fontana said, pointing to an outcropping on the canyon's slope above and in front of them, "and wait for daylight. Then if he rides out of camp we'll be setting where we can pick him off easy as you please."

"If we're real lucky," Charlie Durbin said, still not convinced that it would be a simple task. "Something maybe'll go wrong . . . Looks like they're turning in. Maybe we can get us a better look-see at them now."

"I think it's him all right," Red said watching the two men, vague, dim shapes in the shadows beyond the fire's reach, move to the edge of the small clearing. "One of them's wearing a flat-crowned hat — one of them Kansas kind."

"I reckon that's all the proof we need," Durbin admitted. "We got him where we're wanting him."

Malick swore softly. "You're making too much of a to-do about that jasper. Sure, he's tricky, and I ain't saying he's not fast with that gun of his'n — but I still claim it'd be easy to sneak in close and nail him while he's laying there sleeping."

"You'd never get close enough," Fontana said. "And he'd trick you — outsmart you, somehow —"

"And it being dark'll help him much as it would you," Durbin said.

"Charlie's right," Red added. "Nope, we play it safe and do it like I planned — set back and pick him off."

Gabe's thick shoulders stirred

indifferently, and then abruptly he drew himself up. The woman had risen, was standing at the edge of the fire's glow, her shape fully silhouetted.

"That gal sure looks good from here," the big outlaw said in a hoarse whisper. "I wouldn't mind slipping down there all by myself just to get acquainted."

Fontana, unsure whether Malick meant it or not, but suspecting that he did, whirled quickly.

"Damn you, Gabe — don't you try it!" he said. "Be about the best way of messing up my plans I can think of — save doing what you was wanting to a bit ago. If you're honing for that gal, wait till after we've took care of Rye — understand?"

"Sure," Malick said agreeably. "You're the ramrod of this outfit and what you say goes — but I'm staking my claim on her right now. And something else," he added as Red started to lead the way to the outcropping, "when you start shooting in the morning, be damn sure you don't put no bullet in her!"

Six

Rye was up and about first that next morning, and had begun to throw his gear onto the big chestnut gelding when Patience Chase roused and hurriedly started her breakfast preparations. Such activity stirred Ben into wakefulness and shortly he, too, was on his feet and going about the business of building a fire, not only for cooking purposes but to ease the chill of the crisp, clear air.

That chore completed, Chase stood with his back to the flames, hands clasped behind him as he watched the lawman working with the horse.

"Mighty fine animal you've got there, Marshal," he said after a time.

Rye nodded. He'd had the chestnut for

over a year and was well satisfied with him. "Can't complain. He's done everything I've ever asked of him," he said.

"Could figure he would. Good Morgan blood, can see that. One thing I sure know plenty about is horses. The warden let me take care of —"

Ben's voice trailed off into silence as if he were speaking words he did not wish heard. Nearby, Patience paused, glanced up from the spider in which she was frying salt pork. Rye, however, continued his labors but the woman's startled reaction and the homesteader's statement were not lost to him.

"How long were you in the pen?" he asked a few moments later. Nothing about men surprised him anymore.

Chase, head down, hands still locked behind his back, shrugged, said, "Five years."

"What for?"

"Stealing. Guess I forgot to tell you."

"Yeh, you did," Rye said bluntly, "but it's no business of mine. You broke the law and paid for it with five years of your life."

Patience had returned her attention to the frying meat, was now adding chunks of potatoes left to bake overnight in the coals of the fire. On a flat rock at the edge of the flames biscuits were again being warmed up while the water in the coffeepot suspended nearby was beginning to simmer.

"It ain't something I'm proud of —"

"Glad to hear that," Rye said.

"But it's all behind me now," the homesteader continued. "Big reason we're heading down to Texas. Aim to get a fresh start there."

Crows were streaming raggedly overhead in the clean sky, cawing noisily in their flight, and over in the creek a fish slapped as it rose to an insect. Rye, the good odor of wood smoke mingling with the smells of food being prepared filling his nostrils, paused, looked off down the canyon.

He was never too impressed when hearing outlaws, released from prison, declaring that they intended to make a fresh start. It usually didn't work out that way, and sooner or later, depressed by failure and hardship, they reverted to the old and easy — and lawless — methods of getting money.

There were exceptions, of course, and

for the sake of Patience, he hoped Ben would be counted among those.

"Want to wish you luck," he said. The chestnut was saddled and bridled; the shotgun was in its boot, his blanket roll wrapped and with his slicker, secure against the cantle, and the saddlebags in place. He was ready to ride out. Moving forward out of the brush growing thick along the base of the bluff, he glanced at the woman. By chance she looked up at that exact moment.

"It'll only be a few more minutes," she said. "You men go right on talking."

Rye nodded, dropped to his heels to hunker near the chestnut at the edge of the clearing. Casting another glance at the straggling crows, he said to Ben: "How long did you folks live in Montana?"

"Most of our lives," Chase replied, his gaze also on the lazily flying birds. "Seeing them black pests sort of makes me homesick. Was always having to drive them off when we had the farm. Pa tried rigging up a scarecrow. Didn't bother them a'tall. I sort of got the feeling they thought it was there for them to roost on while they was feeding."

The lawman smiled faintly. "Where's your pa now?"

"Dead — him and Ma both. . . . Where you from, Marshal?"

"Home was in Tennessee. My people had a farm there but the war ruined it the same as it did a lot of others. Went to Texas after Appomattox."

"You fight in the war?"

"Was in the cavalry," Rye said, making no issue of the side for which he fought. It was unnecessary. The soft drawling voice, the rounded edge of certain words, and the location of his birth stamped him as a Southerner.

"You always been a U. S. Marshal — I mean since you took up lawing?"

Rye shook his head. "Spent some time being a deputy sheriff. Had a job for a while riding guard over a bullion wagon."

He might have added that, thanks to his expertise with a pistol, he had also been a bounty hunter, but he let it slide. Like most men of his kind he never relished talking about himself and of his past, thus his answers at such times were always as brief as courtesy permitted.

"It's ready —"

At Patience's announcement, Rye drew himself upright, and, joining Ben, moved to the fire where the woman had filled plates with steaming food and warm biscuits. Taking up one, along with a cup of coffee, he retired to his original place at the fringe of the brush, again squatted on his heels, and began to eat.

He was losing time and it troubled him. Had he been alone he would have ridden out at least a full hour earlier — probably with no breakfast under his belt, of course, but he would have fortified himself with coffee thoroughly boiled while he was readying the chestnut for traveling.

He guessed he'd be able to make it up. The big horse would be in fine fettle after a night's rest, during which he had satisfied himself with plenty of grass and water; he would be in condition for a fast hard run. Anyway, refusing the hospitality of the Chases would have been impolite.

Rye, plate almost cleaned, glanced up as Patience moved to him, a small cloth sack in her hands. As she approached, he came to his feet.

"Some lunch I've fixed for you," she

said, passing the sack to him. "Not much — a little meat, a few biscuits, but it will save you from stopping."

The lawman smiled, nodded, noting that her eyes were a light blue, that her brows were dark and thick. He had been unable to tell much about her in the deceptive glow of the fire that previous night, but daylight confirmed what he had assumed at that time; Patience Chase was a beautiful woman. Ben was a lucky man.

"I'm obliged to you, ma'am," he said formally. "It'll be a big help."

Patience was pleased. It showed in her eyes and in a parting of her lips. "I'm glad. I know that by staying with us you were delayed."

"I'll make it up. . . . Like to thank you again for that meal last night, and the fine one this morning. Were mighty tasty. I'll be remembering them for a long time."

"You aiming to head straight on down the Trail?" Ben asked, setting his empty plate aside and refilling his cup with coffee.

"Man I'm after's somewhere ahead of me, far as I know," the lawman replied, stepping over to his horse and placing the sack of lunch in a saddlebag. "Only thing I can do is keep working on that basis until I either catch up with him, or find out I've been on the wrong track."

"Well, I sure hope you get him," Chase said, taking the empty plate from Rye's hand, along with his drained cup, and adding them to his. "Sure seems like a business where a man follows mighty long shots most of the time."

"Way the cards fall now and then," Rye said, and turned to his horse. Catching up the lines, the lawman came back around, extended his hand to Chase.

"Want to thank you for your hospitality," he said. "Like to again wish you luck, too."

"Thanks. Same goes for you," Ben said.

The marshal moved forward a step to where Patience was waiting, her steady gaze upon him, and offered her his hand.

"I'm thanking you, too, Mrs. Chase. You've been kind, and I appreciate it."

"It was my pleasure," she murmured. "I — I hope we meet again someday."

"Could be," John Rye said, and,

pivoting, thrust a booted foot into a stirrup and swung up onto his horse.

He spent a few moments getting himself set — adjusting his holster, tugging at the wool poncho until it hung loose and comfortable from his broad shoulders, tilting his flat-brimmed hat lower over his eyes that they might be shaded from the sun, and then moved away from the undergrowth into the center of the clearing.

Touching Patience and Ben with his level glance, he roweled the chestnut, and rocking forward slightly on his saddle in further search of comfort, rode quickly out of the pocket of screening brush onto the Trail.

In that exact instant of time gunshots shattered the early morning stillness. Rye felt the searing impact of a bullet ripping into his arm — somewhere below his left shoulder. Instinctively, and cool despite the anger that suddenly filled him, he threw himself from the gelding's back to the ground.

Seven

Pain racing through him, Rye hit solid ground with jarring force. Bullets were striking all around him, sending up geysers of powdery dust, or whining shrilly off rocks. Fortunately the chestnut was between him and the outcropping a short distance up the canyon wall where the bushwhackers appeared to be lodged. The big horse, shying and milling about nervously, was spoiling any good shot they might have at him.

Ignoring his throbbing arm, the lawman rolled clear of the gelding. He was risking the possibility of presenting the killers with an easy target, he knew, but he had to get away from the horse, avoid the animal's trampling hoofs, and reach the brush at the foot of the slope. Once there he could not be seen at all by the bushwhackers.

He gained the brush, and pistol now out, began to throw an answering fire at the killers — men, he assumed, and wondered who in the hell they might be. He had no view of them, could only guess at their exact positions among the rocks and brush which, in actuality, were beyond accurate pistol range.

He had to get nearer. Grim, cold, white anger coursing through him, Rye reloaded his empty weapon, and began to work his way upward through the brush. Powder smoke and dust were hanging over the slope and the Trail in a pale, restless cloud, and the crows, while still passing overhead, had been frightened into silence by the gunfire.

Rye paused, brushing off an unsteadiness, aware suddenly of the quiet. The bushwhackers had ceased shooting. No longer having any idea of where he was they had lowered their rifles to wait and watch — or else were moving out. Moments later Rye heard the thud of hoofs, the rattle of gravel, displaced and cascading down the slope to the shoulder of the Trail below. The outlaws were giving it up.

Grim set, cursing quietly, Rye drew himself erect and hurriedly descended the short distance to the Trail where he had a full view of the canyon. Three men, spurring their horses recklessly across the unstable surface of the slope, were rushing to gain the flat plain above them.

The marshal shaded his eyes with an open hand, endeavored to get a look at them and determine who they were. It wasn't possible. The men were too far away, and hunched over their saddles, backs to him, he could not even guess at their identities.

Again reloading his pistol, Rye slid it back into the holster, and wheeling about, started back for the camp in the clearing. His arm was paining insistently, and his left sleeve and corresponding side of his shirt were soaked with blood, but as before, he ignored all discomfort, considering instead the incident.

Who were the bushwhackers? Why had they sought to kill him? Could one of them be the man who murdered Judge Brite, and now assisted by two friends, was out to get him off his trail? Or were they old enemies out of the past with a grudge gnawing at their guts craving to be satisfied?

"You're hurt — bad!"

Rifle clutched in her hands, and apparently about to be used, Patience Chase met him at the edge of the brush. Her eyes were wide and filled with concern. Beyond her Rye saw Ben. The homesteader had caught the chestnut, was calming him by rubbing the animal's corded neck.

"Only in the arm," the lawman said, and as the woman leaned her weapon against a clump of oak and pointed resolutely at a large stone near the firebed, crossed and sat down. "No need to trouble —"

"There's plenty of need!" the woman snapped. She took one of the small pans, filled it with water and set it over the flames. "Here, let me take that poncho off — it'll get in the way. That shirt, too. I've got to get to that bullet hole."

Silent, Rye complied, assisting her as she removed the necessary clothing. The shirt's sleeve had already stuck to the open wound. Patience murmured something to the effect that she would free it as soon as the water heated; he shook his head impatiently, and reaching across his chest, jerked the fabric clear.

"Now you've started it to bleeding worse!" the woman scolded. "It wouldn't've hurt you to wait."

"I've got no time," he said tautly.

"You'll be taking time whether you like it or not," Patience countered. "You just better make up your mind to that! You've got a nasty wound. The bullet missed the bone — and you can thank your lucky stars for that — but the flesh is torn real bad. Once I get it cleaned and bandaged, you'll have to take it easy — at least for the rest of today, maybe even tomorrow."

"No, ma'am," Rye said, coldly stubborn. "Soon as you're through with your doctoring, I'll be on my way."

"Not likely," Patience replied evenly.

John Rye came suddenly to his feet, temper and frustration having its way with him. "Lady, I'm obliged to you for wanting to help, but I don't have the time to spare! Fact is, I've been hurt a lot worse than this before, and kept going. Expect I can do so again."

"I expect you can," Patience said quietly, and turned toward the fire. "Sit down, please. This won't take long."

The lawman resumed his place on the rock, jaw set, eyes reflecting his impatience and displeasure. The water in the pan over the fire was beginning to steam and, setting it off, Patience obtained a strip of white cloth from the carpetbag in which she carried clothing and various other articles. Ripping off a small square, she shaped it into a pad and began to cleanse the ugly wound.

Ben had led the gelding back to where the other horses were still picketed, secured him, and returned to take up a stand near the fire.

"You needing a cup of coffee?" he asked, pouring out a measure for himself. "Sure sorry we ain't got nothing stronger."

Rye shook his head. "Obliged, anyway."

Ben squatted on his heels, sipped thoughtfully at his drink. Then, "You got any idea who them jaspers was? Sure were hell-bent on killing you."

"I never got close enough to get a look at them. Was three in the bunch and they took off for the mesa above the canyon. About all I can say."

"You reckon one of them could be that killer you're chasing?"

"Good chance of it."

Patience had satisfied herself as to the cleanliness of the wound, and now exchanged the hot water pad for one soaked in cold.

"Need to stop — or slow down — the bleeding," she said more to herself than to Rye or her husband. "Want the blood to clot."

"Expect you're wondering why I didn't grab a gun and give you a hand," Ben said in a tentative voice.

It hadn't occurred to Rye, but now that it had been brought to his attention, he did wonder. Patience had taken up a rifle as if to help; it was a bit strange that Ben Chase had not done likewise, under the circumstances.

"I just ain't no good at shooting," the homesteader said before the lawman could reply. "I'm handy at farming things — grinding oats and corn for the live-stock, splitting and ricking wood — but shooting at another man — I plain ain't got the sand for it."

Rye nodded indifferently, signifying his understanding. He was recalling that Ben Chase had covered over his fire that night rather than draw the attention of anyone on the Trail and bring danger to Patience and himself.

In the light of present action he guessed such had been Ben's idea rather than his wife's, but he made no comment on it.

"Man does best what he's used to," he said.

Patience now had slowed the bleeding of his wound considerably, was preparing a pad with some sort of antiseptic salve coating. Giving him no warning, she placed it on the wound and pressed it tight. Rye swore under his breath, flinched, and then grinned wryly as she began to wind a bandage about his arm.

"There's something to what folks say about a cure being worse than the wound."

Patience returned his smile. "I don't think that's exactly how that saying goes, but I guess I understand what you mean."

"What the hell is that stuff you put on it?"

"A salve Mama showed me how to make. It'll quit burning in a few minutes."

"Kind of like using a red-hot branding iron on a bullet hole to stop the bleeding," the lawman commented.

The woman shivered. Then, "The salve will keep your arm from mortifying."

Rye mumbled something under his breath, stared off into the distance. He was experiencing a bit of light-headedness — from the loss of blood, he supposed. A drink of whiskey would certainly come in handy at that moment — he was a damn fool not to be carrying a bottle; he had in the past, using it for just such an emergency, but it had been a long time since he'd let anyone put a bullet into him and he'd sort of gotten out of the habit. He'd correct that, however. At the very next saloon he came to he'd get a bottle and tuck it away in his saddlebags.

Nodding to Patience, now finished, Rye got to his feet. Again he felt a giddiness, and for an instant or two he swayed uncertainly. At once Patience reached out, took him by his good arm, and led him toward her blanket.

"You're going to sit right there for a spell," she said. "I'll bring you some coffee."

The lawman tried to pull away. "Got no time for this — all foolishness. Best I get my horse, ride on —"

"Later, maybe. Condition you're in now, you'd probably fall off your saddle before you got a half a mile."

They reached the blankets and, pressing hard on his arm, the woman forced him to be seated. That accomplished, she turned to the fire and filled a cup with black, steaming liquid.

"Expect this will do you as much good as liquor, it's so strong," she said.

"Strong because it's chicory," Ben said. "Guess you've already found that out."

Rye nodded. He'd noticed it the night before but since many families could not afford real coffee and were forced to use the root, finely ground, as a substitute, he had refrained from mentioning it.

"Strong's the way I like it," he said, taking a swallow and placing the cup on the ground nearby. "I figure I owe you folks an apology — bringing those outlaws down on you. There was a good chance one of you could've been hit the way those bullets were flying."

"Can't fault you," the homesteader replied. "I don't think they could see us much, anyway, standing back in the brush like we was. Sort of swallowed my teeth when Patience there run out taking my rifle to you — but was all over then so it was all right."

Rye recalled the woman at the edge of the brush, the weapon in her hands. "Want to thank you for that," he said, glancing at her. "Want to say I'm mighty glad neither one of you got hurt."

Patience was adding more fuel to the fire so that the coffee would stay hot. "Do you think they'll still be hanging around?"

"Probably. They know they only winged me — and if they're out to put me in the ground — and I figure they are — they'll try again."

"Why? Why would they want —"

"Ain't hard to explain," Ben Chase said before Rye could reply. "Lawmen've always got a'plenty enemies, and most of them try to get even for something that happened to them or somebody they know — maybe years ago. And then there's them that just plain hate lawmen so much that they shoot them down whenever they get a chance."

Patience listened in silence to Ben's opinion. When he finished she said: "That means you won't have a chance, Marshal — not here, alone. That arm is going to hinder you, keep you from being at your best — and those outlaws know that."

Rye stirred. "Expect I'll manage."

"I doubt that," Patience said in a firm voice. "With them on the loose I think we'd better stay together. Besides that bandage will need changing — and anyway, we'll be going in the same direction."

Rye had to admit to the truth in the woman's statement, although, always a self-sufficient man, he disliked the idea of depending on someone else.

"Don't you think I'm right?" she continued, facing her husband. "Those outlaws could bother us — give us trouble and, well, I'm afraid!"

Chase, head tipped down, considered her words for a long minute, evidently having deep thoughts on the matter. Finally he shrugged.

"Yeh," he said, "we best stick together — at least for a while."

84

Eight

Red Fontana swore wildly as he fought to keep his horse from falling on the steep grade of the slope. The surface was mostly loose gravel and dirt, and had it not been for clumps of weeds and occasional imbedded rocks jutting forth, they would have gone down for sure. Ahead of him Malick and Charlie Durbin were having similar problems.

Everything had gone wrong — and the three of them had turned tail and took off up the canyon like a bunch of renegade Indians with the U.S. Cavalry after them. He had been the one farthest out in the rocks and thus had the best view of John Rye when he rode out of the coulee into the open.

But just as he triggered his rifle the lawman moved. The bullet meant to smash into his chest had instead hit him in the arm, or maybe the shoulder, Red couldn't be sure which. One thing was certain — it was no fatal wound as Rye was on his feet mighty damned quick and coming up the slope after them!

It seemed to him that either Gabe or Charlie could have put a bullet in the marshal if they'd been paying mind to their business. Of course that horse of Rye's had messed things up plenty, moving around, blocking the lawman, keeping them all from getting a decent shot off. He reckoned he couldn't really blame Charlie and Gabe, but still —

And then the next thing Rye had moved clean out of sight and was opening up on them. Bullets came plenty close, too, hitting the rocks where they all three were hiding and glancing off into space. For a bit it looked like the horses were going to get loose and run for it, being so scared. That was when he hollered for the others to pull out, and they all did.

But that wasn't the last verse to the song, no, sir, not by a damn sight! There were a lot of miles of trail yet down which

Mister John Rye had to travel, and all bunged up now with a crippled arm, he shouldn't be such great shucks when the chance came again to take care of him.

Maybe . . . Fontana, face blanketed with sweat, horse blowing hard under him as they gained the top of the canyon wall and broke out onto the flat, grinned in spite of himself. Rye — even if he had two crippled arms — would still be about as dangerous as a cornered grizzly.

"I ain't never seen nobody as lucky as that bastard!" Gabe Malick said, cutting his exhausted horse about to where he could face Fontana. "He's one of them kind that could fall in a hog trough and come out smelling sweet as honey! We had him dead to rights back there!"

Charlie Durbin mopped at his neck, pulled off his hat and ran fingers through his hair. "I ain't so sure it's luck," he said dolefully. "No matter what, things always turn out in his favor. He's just got the knack of ending up on top."

"No, that ain't it at all," Fontana said. "We wasn't scattered out like I wanted —"

"Dammit, Red, you didn't tell —"

"I know. Reckon I forgot — things just

sort of heading up sudden, like they did. The next time it'll be different. We're going to be strung out so's there won't be no chance of us all missing —"

"Didn't miss," Gabe Malick cut in hotly. "Was that horse of his, jumping around there in front of him. Wasn't no chance to —"

"I know that," Fontana said irritably. "Was there, too, right out in front. Damn it all, we sure should've had him!"

"He could've had us," Durbin said, "if he'd a been carrying a rifle instead of a six-gun. Could've picked us off like he was busting beer bottles while we was climbing that slope."

"He dang near did have," Malick said. "Last time I looked back that pilgrim gal was taking a rifle to him. If she'd a done it a couple of jumps earlier we might not've made it to the top."

"But she didn't," Red stated, "so maybe we've got a little luck working for us."

"Can use some," Durbin said glumly. "What're we doing next?"

"We get set again, that's what. I ain't quitting till that tin star's dead!"

Malick rubbed at his jaw. "Going to

be hard catching him by surprise from up here now —"

"Ain't aiming to — not from up here!" Fontana snapped. "It'd be a dumb stunt because he'll be looking for us to try again, and him and that pilgrim'd be waiting for us. We'll make another try, for sure, only it'll be on down the Trail a ways, in a good place that'll suit us — and this time I ain't going to let nothing mess things up. . . . Let's go."

Nine

"You about ready to move out?" Rye asked, endeavoring to control the impatience in his voice. Every moment lost now, he felt, was costing him dearly.

"Wouldn't it be better to hold back for a while, let those outlaws —"

"Makes no difference," the lawman said, cutting into Patience's faint protest. "Could be they'll ride on, and there's just as good a chance they'll be waiting a half a mile down the Trail for us."

Ben, about finished with saddling their two horses, paused. "Kind of puts us between a rock and a hard place. Ain't there nothing we can do?"

"Keep in the brush as much as we can and stay off the high places. Need to watch sharp."

Chase swore quietly. "Going to make it hard going for us."

"What I'm trying to tell you," Rye said curtly. "Best I head out alone."

"No!" Patience cried in an urgent voice. "Maybe you don't think you need us — but I think we need you — at least until we can reach civilization. I can't bear the thought of being out here alone —"

"You ain't hardly alone," Ben said stiffly. "Happens I'll be with you."

"I know that," Patience replied, "and I don't mean to say you're not a man — a good man, but you're no match for those outlaws; you've said so yourself. You're a farmer, not a gunfighter. We need someone like the marshal."

Rye said nothing, but he could understand her fear. Chase had demonstrated his inability to face up to trouble by trying to dodge it. And earlier, when the outlaws had opened up on him, the homesteader had failed to even draw his gun.

"We'll be ready soon, Marshal," the woman said then, making the decision. "Sit down, rest your arm all you can while you've got the chance. It will bother you plenty when you start riding."

The lawman shrugged. Patience talked as if he'd never been shot before; hell, he had at least a dozen scars to show where bullets and knives had found him at various times during his life! But Patience meant well, and, when it came right down to bedrock, it was kind of nice having a woman fret over him a little.

Shortly the Chases were ready to leave, and Rye, mounting the chestnut, cutting about and heading back through the brush on the west side of the clearing, led the way to the arroyo. It would provide the safest course to follow, having a good stand of scrub oak, Juneberry, and sumac growing along its banks that would screen their passage.

Rye kept to the head of the column, ignoring the throbbing in his arm while maintaining a close watch on the ragged slopes to either side as well as on the wash ahead. The sun was out and well on its way across the clean, blue heaven by then, and the chill had gradually left the air. In only a brief time Rye removed the poncho and added it to the roll behind the saddle's cantle. The Chases, too, soon discarded their heavy jackets.

The day wore on with no sign of the outlaws. Late in the morning the hills began to flatten out, the sandy-floored arroyo with its concealing brush down which they had come disappeared, and abruptly they were out on a wide, grassy mesa populated here and there with stands of piñon and juniper trees. At once Patience and Ben drew up alongside the lawman.

"Is there a town somewhere around here?" the woman asked.

Rye shook his head. "Stranger to this part of the country myself, so I couldn't tell you. Seems there should be, though. We cross the Platte River farther on. Can just about figure on there being a settlement there."

"How much farther will that be?" she wondered aloud.

"Can't tell you that, either. Near as I recollect the map I saw, we ought to reach it by dark — but that's only guessing."

They moved on steadily, occasionally passing through bands of brush and small groves of trees, but mostly out in flat, open country. Around midday Rye called a halt in a cluster of oaks where a spring bubbled forth to form a shallow pond.

They ate of the lunch Patience quickly prepared, foregoing coffee since it would require a fire — and a fire meant telltale smoke that could pinpoint their location for the outlaws, if they were searching.

Rye allowed the horses an abbreviated hour's rest, time that eased the pain in his arm as well, and then they moved on, his impatience at being compelled to travel slowly and continually on the alert rankling deeply. Alone he would have taken less precaution and thereby covered the miles much faster. He would be as thankful as Patience when they reached a town where the Chases would be safe and he could go on about the job of running down Orson Brite's murderer.

A while later Rye spotted dust on the flat off to the east. It appeared too distant to be the outlaws. They would hardly have gotten that far off the Trail. He dismissed any thoughts of danger after a bit deciding it was probably a party of pilgrims heading for Kansas.

Near the middle of the afternoon, with the horses again lagging and Patience near exhaustion from the continual riding, the marshal drew up again, this time in the shade of a low, solitary butte. There was no stream or spring convenient and the brush was thin, but it would afford the woman and Ben, who was also showing saddle weariness, to stretch their legs and ease their aching muscles.

"You think there's for sure a town on up ahead?" Chase asked, walking slowly about in a circle.

At the moment the lawman's attention was fixed on two distant figures shimmering eerily in the layers of heat hovering over the flat, as they bore steadily north. Pilgrims, he concluded; they'd have no connection with him and his problems.

"Not certain of anything," he said, answering the homesteader's question. He thought he'd made that bit of information clear earlier. "But where trails cross somebody usually builds a store — or a saloon — and if it does any good, others come in and set up for business and pretty soon you've got a town."

"Then you figure there's a crossroad

on a ways —"

Rye pointed to the cloud of dust to the east. "One somewhere. Can't say it'll be crossing this Trail any time soon, however. Could be close."

Chase, now squatting on his heels in the shadow of the stubby formation, shrugged, stared out over the prairie land.

"Looks like we got all worked up over them outlaws for nothing. If they was aiming to make another try at you — or us, they would've done it by now."

Rye nodded. "Probably right."

"You could've gone on alone — like you was wanting to do. Can see that it galls you to be riding slow — and you're doing that on account of us. If you're of a mind, Marshal, why, go on. We'll make it all right now."

"I don't think he should," Patience said hurriedly, worry filling her eyes. "I — I still don't feel that it's safe — and anyway, we can't be too far from a town."

"If there is one," Ben said.

"I know — there's nothing for sure, but we've come miles and miles with nothing along the way so it's only reasonable to think we'll reach a settlement soon.''

Rye took no part in the discussion. He would prefer, of course, to accept Ben Chase's offer and ride on, but he wasn't convinced that the outlaws had given up and departed the area; and there was no doubt that Patience was in mortal fear of them moving in on her and Ben and their being at their mercy.

He couldn't subject her to such fear, and if his being with her and her husband filled her with a feeling of security, then he reckoned he could restrain his impatience and content himself with the delay. It could mean he would run into considerable difficulty in tracking down Brite's killer — but on the other hand he could look forward to many sleepless nights, he knew, if after leaving the Chases they became victims of the outlaws.

''I guess it's up to you, Marshal,'' Ben said.

''It's best we stay together,'' Rye replied, settling the matter, ''at least till we get to a place where you can join up with other pilgrims going your way. Maybe it won't be far.''

The sigh of relief escaping Patience was clearly audible. "Thank you," she murmured as her eyes filled with gratitude.

Ten

The name of the settlement — no more than a general store, saloon, and livery stable all in one ramshackle, rambling building — was Cow Springs. As Rye had thought, it was on the Platte River, although there was no sign of a cross-road.

They reached there, still without seeing any indication of the outlaws, late in the afternoon, and halted at the edge of the flat upon which the structure, enlarged, evidently, in piecemeal fashion, was built. Rye considered the assemblage narrowly, thinking the outlaws might have chosen the place for a second ambush, but from where they had stopped, Cow Springs was fully visible and he could see nothing to arouse his suspicion.

"It sure ain't much," he heard Ben say.

The lawman agreed. The place looked bleak, the unpainted boards of the buildings cracked and warped by the elements, and with no signs of life, all appeared deserted. The Chases were no better off here than they were thirty miles back up the Arapaho Trail, he realized. He might as well accept the fact that he'd continue to be saddled with them for time to come.

"Over here — folks!" a voice shouted from the entrance to the general store. "I'm Grover Gillette. You're welcome to come in out of the sun."

"We staying the night here?" Ben asked. "Horse of mine's got a loose shoe. Want to fix it before we go on."

Rye glanced around. Cow Springs was no place to stop over; it offered nothing and could prove an attraction to the outlaws, should they be nearby.

"Take care of it," Rye said, jerking his thumb toward the stable, "then meet us at the store. I've got a hunch we'll be better off making camp down the Trail a ways."

"There's some things I should buy — groceries, I mean," Patience said.

"Looks like Gillette has some stock," the lawman said. "Maybe you can find what you want in his store."

They moved on, Ben veering to the livery barn with its extended open roof beneath which there was a forge and other blacksmith tools, Rye and the woman continuing to the hitch rack fronting the mercantile section of the establishment.

Grover Gillette, a narrow-faced little man with small, darting black eyes and a slyness about him, met them at the sagging screen door, holding it wide for them to enter. As Patience passed by him he reached out, touched her on the arm.

"You're a mighty pretty lady," he said, and hurriedly bowed to Rye. "No offense, mister! And I want to say you're a lucky man to have a fine-looking woman like her for a wife."

The lawman's shoulders stirred as he cradled his throbbing arm with a free hand. "She's not my wife," and as Gillette's face lit up eagerly, shook his head. "Husband's that big fellow out there in your stable getting a loose shoe on his horse fixed.''

"Ain't no smithy around,'' Gillette said, watching Patience move by him and deeper into the dusty room. "Just me. I run the whole shooting match — own it, in fact.''

Patience paused in her survey of the thinly stocked shelves. "You live here all alone?''

"I sure do, lady! My woman up and died on me near five year ago. Sure does get lonesome, I can tell you!''

Gillette's features had taken on an oily shine. The lawman considered him narrowly for a long moment. Then, "You had any customers in the last day or two?''

The storekeeper did not take his eyes off Patience Chase, now halted in front of a short counter in the back room.

"Nope, ain't been nobody come in.''

"What about riders passing through — a man by himself.''

Gillette shook his head. "Nope —''

"A bunch of three men?''

"Nope —''

Rye, suddenly out of patience, seized the storekeeper by the shoulder, jerked him roughly around.

"Damn it — pay attention and listen to me! I'm a lawman. I'm looking for a man who could've been riding by himself, headed south — or maybe he was with three other men. They had to pass by here. Now think again — did you see any of them?"

Gillette bobbed anxiously and an apologetic sort of smile cracked his thin lips. "Well, yeh, reckon I did. Leastwise, I recollect hearing horses —"

"When?" Rye pressed.

Grover Gillette's eyes were again on Patience, devouring her hungrily. "Was yesterday, or maybe it was this morning around noon."

"Which was it — the man by himself or the three riders?"

"I can't be sure. Wasn't nobody stopped —"

"Headed which way?"

"Towards the ford — anyway it sounded like that was it. . . . What can old Grover get you, little lady?" the storekeeper said and moved over to Patience.

"I'm going over to the saloon," Rye called after the man. "Need a little whiskey. I pay for it here?"

Gillette was only slightly interested. "Just help yourself, then come pay me here," he said.

The lawman pivoted on a heel, returned to the front landing of the store, and moved off for the door over which was the faded sign reading SALOON. His arm had never ceased paining and he was looking forward to a drink or two of whiskey in hopes that it would help.

The interior of the saloon, no more than a narrow room with a crude plank bar behind which was a single shelf supporting a half-a-dozen bottles, was almost totally dark. Rye, striking a match, looked along the brief row of bottles until he found one that was near full — there being none that were yet unopened. It was a quart, far more than he needed or desired, but he pulled the cork and treated himself to a long swallow. Then, holding the bottle by its neck, he restored the cork and retreated through the darkness to the landing.

The lawman halted there, seemingly already feeling the effects of the liquor, and threw his glance to the livery stable. Ben, wearing the smithy's leather apron, had the right foreleg of his horse folded and caught between his knees and was nailing the shoe back into place. The homesteader was about finished, Rye saw, as would be Patience by then; they should be on their way in another quarter hour.

Opening the screen door, Rye stepped inside, halted. A frown pulled at the flat planes of his face. Neither Patience nor Gillette was there. Setting the whiskey on a nearby shelf, he walked farther into the room. On the counter at the back of the store were several items apparently selected by the woman — dry onions, potatoes, baking powder, salt, a can of tomatoes, and a few odds and ends — but there was no evidence of her or of the storekeeper.

The faint sound of scuffling reached the lawman. It came from beyond a door in the wall back of the counter, apparently Gillette's living quarters. An oath ripped from John Rye's throat. In a dozen strides he circled the counter and reached the scarred panel. Ignoring the knob, he booted it open.

In the rear of the littered combination bedroom and kitchen, Gillette had

Patience crowded into a corner. He was pinning her against the wall with his body; the fingers of one hand were locked in her hair to hold her head rigid, and as he struggled to kiss her, his other hand was fumbling with the buttons of her shirt.

The woman, face flushed, eyes spread wide, was doing her best to fight off the man, get free. When she saw Rye enter, she managed a breathless cry, but the lawman, anger surging through him, was already crossing the room.

Gillette seemed unaware of Rye's presence. The lawman, forgetting his injured arm in his fury, caught the storekeeper by the shoulder, jerked him clear of the woman, and drove a fist to the side of his head. Gillette went to his knees as Patience hurried away, escaping to the opposite side of the room.

Relentless, Rye dragged the man upright, again without thought using his injured arm, and smashed him once more with a knotted fist. The storekeeper bounced back against the wall with such force that the impact dislodged articles on a shelf close by and sent them tumbling to the floor.

106

Coolly methodic, Rye caught the man by the throat, raised him to a sagging stance, and, holding him there against the wall, cocked his arm for another blow.

"I ought to kill you," he said in a carefully controlled voice.

Gillette raised a restraining hand, held it in front of his face, now showing a dark area where the lawman's sledging knuckles had connected.

"I didn't mean nothing — for sure I didn't!" the man said. "Just that I ain't seen a woman for so long, maybe near a year now — and this'n's so pretty, I lost my head."

"He told me he had some fresh vegetables out on his back porch. Was keeping them there so they wouldn't spoil," Patience, straightening her clothing and pushing her hair back into place, explained. "I went with him to pick out some but when we got in here he slammed the door and tried to push me down on the bed. I got away from him but then he grabbed me and threw me into that corner. I kept fighting him and trying to get loose — was doing my best when I saw you come in."

"I didn't mean to hurt —" Gillette began, but his words ended abruptly when Rye once more slammed him into the wall.

"I think the thing to do is tell the lady's husband about this," the lawman said, releasing his grip on the man and stepping back. "He's got the right to take care of you — any way he wants."

The storekeeper moaned, rubbed at the back of his head. "Ain't you already done enough to me? Why don't you just go on — take what you want. Ain't no need to pay."

Rye turned his attention to Patience. "It's up to you, ma'am. You want me to tell Ben about this?"

The woman shook her head. "Let it pass. I just want to get out of here — forget him —"

The lawman nodded, reached into his pocket. Taking out a handful of coins, he followed Patience Chase into the store area, and while she was collecting her purchases and dropping them into a flour sack, he laid several silver dollars on the counter.

"You're getting paid for what we're taking," he called back to the storekeeper. "If there's any argument about the amount, I'll be coming through here again and we can straighten it out."

"Won't be no need," Grover Gillette replied in a falling voice. "Just take what you want and get out."

Patience, groceries in her arms, hurried toward the front door. Rye, pausing long enough to retrieve his bottle of whiskey, was close behind. His injured arm was now paining him intensely, and there was a wetness to the wound.

Patience noted the strained expression of his features, drew up short. "Your arm — it's started to bleed again!" she cried. "I'll get some cold water — see if I can stop —"

"Later — after we get away from here," Rye cut in, his voice tight.

Patience glanced to the stable. "All right. Ben's coming so we can go."

Eleven

— They rode south for a full hour, after fording the river, halting on the banks of a small creek when the day began to die. A deep silence had sprung up among them, each being occupied by personal thoughts. Patience, no doubt, was reliving the frightening moments in Grover Gillette's store; Ben, perhaps, was thinking of the future he hoped to find in Texas, while John Rye fumed inwardly at the delays being forced upon him.

It irritated him to be in a position of having to proceed with care, to literally be dodging the three men who were trying to kill him. Ordinarily such would call for him setting out immediately in pursuit, tracking them down and settling the matter with his gun.

But this time it was different — he couldn't handle the situation in his usual direct fashion. He was charged with the task of bringing in the killer of Orson Brite and personal problems must wait, thus he could do nothing but continue the search for the murderer, who could be one of the outlaws, and try to stay alive.

That, in itself, was slowing him down far too much, but add to such the care of the two greenhorns with whom he had become saddled and he supposed he should consider himself fortunate that the pursuit had not come to a complete standstill.

Going about the chore of unsaddling the chestnut and exchanging the bridle for a halter which allowed the horse to graze with more ease, Rye's thoughts centered on Patience and Ben Chase.

He guessed he shouldn't call them greenhorns, thereby relegating them to the class of persons who were nothing but trouble on the Trail. Both had lived on the frontier all of their lives and knew pretty well how to take care of themselves under most conditions.

That did not include coping with the hardcase outlaws they were certain to encounter as they traveled across country, however. In a thinly populated land where women were scarce — and attractive ones like Patience were a rarity — the husband of one such as her was in for trouble. His wife would be a much sought after prize and he'd best be ready to stand and fight for her at any time. It seemed to the lawman that Ben Chase lacked both the will and the interest to do so, although he clearly recognized the danger.

A thought occurred to John Rye at that moment: could it be the three outlaws who had jumped them early that morning were not out to kill him specifically but were after Patience?

True he had been the one that a bullet had found, but that was because Ben had not moved out to where he could be seen. Perhaps the would-be killers were not enemies out of the past after all; maybe they were only ordinary outlaws forced to keep to the hills in order to avoid the law, and who were hungry for women.

Patience hadn't forgotten Rye's wound. When he had bedded the chestnut for the night and turned back into the camp, she met him at the fire, one already built and burning brightly under a pan of water.

"I want to change that dressing again," she said, pointing to a log that Ben had dragged up to serve as a bench. "Sit down there."

The lawman frowned. "You did that back at the river —"

"I just stopped the bleeding," she said patiently. "Time now for a fresh dressing."

Rye shrugged resignedly, settled himself on the log. Nearby Ben had brought up more wood for the night, was now unloading the flour sacks in which grub and the utensils for preparing it were carried, and placing them near the stone-banked fire box where they would be convenient for his wife.

"I don't think I thanked you for what you did back there in that store," Patience said in a low voice as she removed the stained bandage.

"No need," the lawman replied. Then, "Still think it would've been a good idea to let your husband teach him a lesson."

She seemed not to hear the latter words. "Thank you just the same, Marshal — I can't remember ever being so frightened." She paused there as if reconsidering, added, "I thank you, too, for not saying anything to him about it."

Puzzled, Rye said: "Why? It was his right to know, or were you scared he might kill Gillette?"

Patience brushed a stray lock of hair from her eyes with her forearm. "No, I don't think he'd do that, not that he isn't capable of it — it's just that I'm not sure he'd look at what happened in the same light as you do."

"You mean he wouldn't get all riled up if he found out some jasper forced himself on you and tried —"

"Yes, I guess that's what I mean," Patience broke in. The old bandage was off and she was now cleaning the wound of crusted bits of blood.

Rye swore softly under his breath. "It's a little hard to believe that. If I had a wife like you, I expect any man who pulled that on her would wind up dead."

Patience, her smooth, soft features flushing slightly, nodded. "Yes, I guess he would."

"Goes for most men I know, too. They'd not stand for anything like that."

"No, I suppose not. Do you have a wife, Marshal?"

"Sure don't."

"Someone that means a lot to you — a sweetheart?"

"No —"

"Haven't you ever been married?" The wound had been cleaned to her satisfaction, a fresh pad coated with stinging antiseptic had been applied, and the woman was now winding the new bandage about his arm.

"No, never found the time, I guess. Doubt if a marriage would ever work out, anyway. Job I've got keeps me on the move most all the time. Been that way ever since I got out of the Army."

Patience had finished. She settled back and, hands clasped together, studied him soberly. Then, "It must be a lonely world you live in, Marshal — never long in one place, no family, no one to go home to — only friends —"

"Can't say that I've got many of them running around, either," Rye said with a grin.

"I can understand why. Ben told me about you, about you being the man they all called the Doomsday Marshal. He said just about every man in the prison where he was knew you — or knew about you."

"Can hardly call any of them friends," the lawman said dryly.

"I — I didn't mean that —"

Rye's shoulders stirred. "Not many folks outside the walls who'd invite me home to supper, either. There's something about a lawman that makes folks pull away — like they didn't want to be seen cozying up to a man wearing a star."

Patience was frowning, staring at him. "I didn't realize people felt that way! I can hardly believe it!"

"I'm not saying everybody does, but it's true most of the time. Never bothers me because I can see their point — they're scared some outlaw might spot them getting friendly with me and turn on them someday."

Shaking her head slowly, Patience said: "Being a lawman must be even more lonely than I thought."

"Never noticed it —"

"Well, I would think it would be nicer

for you if you had a home and a family to go to when you had finished with the job you were doing."

"Might be, but in this business a man's a fool to make any plans — he knows it's best to take things a day at a time. And he'd be a bigger fool to bring a woman in on that kind of a deal. He'd just be letting her in for a lot of grief and worry."

"She'd not mind if she loved him," Patience said. "It would be a part of being married."

John Rye shifted on the log. He didn't particularly like the topic of conversation. He'd long since closed out the idea of a woman becoming a permanent part of his life for the very reasons he'd outlined to Patience, and he ordinarily avoided discussing it.

It was not that he had anything against women; he appreciated them as much as any man and had spent many enjoyable hours in their company as he crossed and recrossed the country — but it was always a fleeting one-night kind of friendship. He refused, flatly, to get himself involved in any lasting relationship.

"How about fixing a bite to eat?"

Ben's voice cut into their thoughts. Patience, collecting her medical supplies, rose, smiled at Rye.

"Expect you're hungry, too."

"Eating's a little like friends to me, never let either one get too big in my mind," the lawman said, and as the woman moved off, he shifted his glance to Chase. "Figured to help you set up camp but seems you've got it done."

"Wasn't much to do," Ben replied. "How's the arm?"

"Stiff. . . . I've been hurt worse."

"I'll bet you have. Wasn't much use of us staying over in that town — Cow Springs or whatever it was called — like we was aiming to do."

Rye said, "No, best we keep on going. Bound to be a settlement where you can get lined up for Texas somewhere ahead."

The smell of piñon wood smoke in the cool night air was pleasant and friendly. Patience, the meal over, food stock stored away in sacks suspended above ground where varmints could not get to it, sat on her blanket and stared into the fire. Directly across Ben lay stretched lengthwise to the flames, and beyond him, barely visible in the shadows of the brush, sat John Rye. A bit earlier Patience had watched the play of the flames on his features; they had appeared chiseled, and the glow had turned them to bronze.

Shifting her eyes, she fell to studying him again. He had dropped the poncho over his shoulders, covering his torso but leaving his arms visible. His black, flat-crowned, straight-brimmed hat was tipped slightly forward over his eyes, and the long, thin cigar he was smoking was clamped in a corner of his mouth.

Just after eating Ben had shared a drink from the bottle of whiskey Rye had bought in Cow Springs. Rye had first offered the liquor to her, out of sheer politeness, she knew, and when she'd declined there'd been a glint of approval in his perpetually narrowed eyes.

The whiskey hadn't affected him to any extent, she noted, it neither loosened his tongue nor tightened it to any greater degree than usual. His manner was no less unbending and she guessed he was a man careful with spirits and who never permitted himself to overindulge in any way.

It would be in accord with his nature. He was one who never really let down his guard, one forever cautious and on the alert. She supposed that stemmed from the kind of life he led. No man could spend his days and nights in pursuit of and dealing with the worst outlaws without building up a sort of constantly vigilant outlook.

That was all to the good. Undoubtedly the enemy of many outlaws, such as the three who had tried to kill him that morning, he needed to be on the watch for such attempts. What would it be like to live with a man burdened with such a problem?

Would it be exciting? Thrilling? Or would it be as he had said — a life of continual worry, never knowing for certain if he was all right or was lying somewhere in the hills badly wounded in need of help — or maybe dead.

Patience, considering it, decided it would make no difference to her if he was her husband. She'd have enough faith in him and his ability to know that he'd survive even the most violent of incidents and return safely to her at the proper time. She'd not worry and fret over him as perhaps an ordinary wife who did not know him well would do.

Did she really know him all that well? Covertly, Patience again fell to studying him in the flickering light of the fire. He had scarcely stirred since he'd sat down. The dust-blanketed hat was still tipped forward but now she could see the dark, heavy line of his brows, the shadowy caverns of his light blue, almost gray eyes; the line of his nose, the crescent of mustache that curved down over his mouth, and the faint shine of the stubble that covered his jaw.

It was a strong, vivid picture that, within the space of but a few moments, was being etched on her mind, and the thought came to her that no matter what the future held, it would always be there.

She stirred, frowned as realization flooded through her suddenly. Love . . . There had been times in the past when she'd believed herself to be in love, but those occasions paled now when confronted by the turmoil that was currently churning within her and causing her heart to swell and pound. This, unquestionably, was the real thing!

"Oh, God," she murmured in a desolate voice and, turning away, began to prepare her bed.

Twelve

Patience's meal that evening was simple but satisfying, and when it was over, Rye, as was his way, complimented her. She had smiled, said something about doing much better if she had more to work with, and gone on about her chores.

The lawman, pulling on his poncho as protection against the increasing coolness of the coming night, and hanging the shotgun in the crook of his right arm, moved off to have a thorough look around the camp, sizing up the possibilities of the three outlaws, or any others who might happen by, closing in unnoticed. He concluded that he and his companions were located in as safe a place as they were likely to find.

It would be prudent, of course, to take no chances, and that called for being constantly on the alert while keeping as much in the shadows as they could. He doubted now that Ben and Patience were in any danger from shots that might originate from a distance, as had been the case that morning; the three outlaws, he was convinced, now that he'd thought it over, were out to get him.

But he warned the Chases, nevertheless, suggesting they not remain too long in the fire's glow and that they make their beds near the brushy overhangs where they would be less noticeable.

As for himself, he dropped his blanket beside a fairly large rock that was all but concealed by a clump of broad-leafed bushes. From there he had an open view to the south and east. If the trio looking to kill him came again, odds were they'd come from one of those directions, he felt.

Satisfied, finally, that he had taken all precautions possible under the circumstances, Rye, the pain in his arm scarcely noticeable, sat down on his bedding and struck a match to a stogie, after first offering one to Chase. The homesteader had declined the weed with a shake of his head and, propped on an elbow, he lay sprawled nearby.

Shortly before they'd had a drink from the bottle of whiskey Rye had provided, and now the tall man seemed strangely withdrawn, as if the liquor had served to still his tongue.

It was a beautiful quiet night, with the black sky littered with stars — angels carrying candles he'd heard a mother explain to her child once — and the land seemed far removed from the violence that, in truth, was always just barely beneath its surface. But that was the way of things and a man took it as it came; there was no way he could change the world to suit himself, and it was only wise to make the best of it.

"What do you aim to do when you get to Texas?" the lawman asked, directing the question to Ben.

Chase stirred, idly selected a bit of wood from the pile close by, and tossed it into the fire. "Got relatives there — ranch people. Figure to go to work for them."

"Good country for it, at least most of

it is," Rye commented. Back to the north of them, coyotes were tuning up, their discordant yapping breaking the hush.

Chase seemed disinclined to state just where in Texas he and Patience would be settling, apparently having some good reason of his own, and the marshal did not press the matter.

"Worked in Texas quite a bit," he said. "Time ever comes when I'm ready to quit, that's the place I'll head for, I expect."

"I'll bet you never take off your star," Ben said. "Always heard that once a fellow becomes a lawman, he never lets go of it."

"And usually dies with his star on — I've heard that, too," Rye said. "Could be true."

"Is that how you feel about it?" Patience asked, folding her blanket into a cushion and sitting down opposite him across the fire.

Rye shrugged, puffed on his cigar. "Something else I've never thought about. Too busy staying alive, I reckon. That's the hard part of being a lawman — dying is easy."

Ben sat up, scrubbed at his jaw. "You

mind if I have another swallow of that whiskey?"

The lawman shook his head. Leaning to one side he took the bottle from his saddlebags, tossed it to Chase, who caught it, pulled the cork, and tipped the neck to his lips for a long drink.

"Obliged," he said, passing the liquor back to Rye. "Tastes mighty good."

The marshal nodded. He was a bit surprised at Ben Chase. Earlier the homesteader had made it clear he had no use for hard liquor — did not hold with it, he had said. A change had come over him, it would seem, and he was taking his drinks in generous quantities.

Chase fell silent once more after that, began to doze in the warmth of the fire's glow. Patience, too, had nothing to say, and several times Rye caught her studying him, and he had his wonder as to what was passing through her mind.

A bit later, when the flames began to dwindle, Ben drew himself up, wrapped his blanket about himself, and again stretching out, went to sleep. Not long after that, Rye, dozing himself, dead cigar clamped between his teeth, heard Patience mutter something, and then she, too, retired.

He relit the stogie, satisfied himself with a few more puffs, and then tossed it into the fire and prepared his blanket. After placing his weapons within easy reach, he stretched out and made himself as comfortable as possible.

The wound in his arm, dormant those past minutes and now disturbed by the activity, began to throb. Hoping to allay the pain, Rye sat up, again took the bottle of liquor from the saddlebags and had a swallow.

It did seem to ease the throbbing, and, lying back after a few minutes, he soon began to doze once more. Schooled in a world of danger, the lawman did not fall entirely asleep, but as was the way of men of his kind, remained suspended in that quiet void of halfway — a state in which he could rest while still being on the alert for any untoward sounds or movements that would herald trouble.

Near midnight he sat up abruptly, the drumming of a running horse having brought his senses to quick attention. Rising, he hung his gun belt over a shoulder and moved silently to the edge of the camp, eyes and ears attuned to the quiet, star-studded night.

He was standing there motionless, a tall shape silhouetted against the darkness, when a soft scraping brought him around — his gun leaping into his hand as if alive.

It was Patience Chase. She jerked back in fear as he whirled upon her, and then as his taut frame relaxed and a hard smile cracked his lips, she came on toward him. Patience had taken her blanket, gathered it about her slim shape leaving only her face visible.

"I — I couldn't sleep — and I thought I heard horses," she began.

"Got me up, too," the lawman said, and paused. "Don't hear it now. Reckon it was some cowhand on the move."

Patience pushed the blanket off her head, allowed her hair to fall free about her shoulders. In the pale light the thick folds appeared corn-yellow, and now as she considered him with direct, serious frankness, her eyes, too, seemed to have changed their color and become darker.

"I hope that's who it was," she murmured. The coyotes were going at full strength, filling the night with their barking. She listened briefly, and then continued. "I'd hate to think it was those outlaws coming back to kill you. The way they hide — in ambush — and shoot at you with rifles, I don't see how they can fail to hit —"

"They always have," Rye interrupted in a kind voice, "that is, they've never done much more than just wing me."

She frowned. "Likely there are outlaws trying all the time to kill you."

Rye shifted his wounded arm, aching dully again, hung it by a thumb from his shirt pocket in an improvised sling.

"Could be. I'll have to say there's a'plenty who'd like to do the job. Where I'm in luck is there's not too many with enough sand to try. Killing a lawman — any lawman — is bad business, and they know it."

"I suppose your reputation, too, holds them back."

"Could have something to do with it — but I never heard of anybody's reputation stopping a bullet."

Patience turned her head, looked off into the night. "You always joke about things like that. Is it your way of never facing up to getting killed?"

The lawman smiled. "There's nothing

gained by fretting about it. You cross a bridge when you come to it, not back down the road a ways."

The woman continued to stare off into the half dark while the coyote chorus maintained its eerie serenade. Finally she came about, faced him.

"I guess I'd be worried about you after all."

Rye frowned, rubbed at his jaw, puzzled. "Not sure I savvy what you mean."

A wry smile parted her lips. "It's nothing," she said, and again looked away.

He remembered then scraps of their earlier conversation, quickly strung them together, and her words took on meaning.

"You're handing me a mighty big compliment," he said, "and I thank you. It would be comforting to have a wife like you worrying over me the way you'd worry over Ben."

John Rye had suddenly realized he was trapped on shaky ground being trod by a married woman — thus the gentle reminder that she had a husband. But he knew also that he best move carefully.

"Like I said," he added, "it's something I'd never put a woman through."

"Even if you meant so much to her that she wouldn't mind?"

"I can't see where that'd make any difference. She still —"

"It would, John," Patience cut in. "Believe me, it would."

Rye straightened. Hearing her call him by his given name, conscious of the urgency in her voice, he felt something deep within him stir — and just as quickly let it die. Patience belonged to another man; she might as well be on another planet.

"Breeze coming up," he said. "Afraid you're going to get cold out here."

Patience was motionless for a long breath and then, nodding woodenly, turned away, an air of hopelessness, of defeat in her manner as she started to retrace her steps.

"Good night," he called after her.

She did not reply, and the lawman, unmoving in the pale night, continued to watch until she had rounded the first bulge of brush and was lost to sight.

He knew well what she had been thinking and what was troubling her, but for the sake of both, he felt it wise to feign ignorance. And while he could never reveal it to her, Patience had evoked kindred feelings within him — something he could not recall any woman he'd met in the past having done.

The situation was simply impossible. She was already married and, being so, the strict code that Rye observed placed her beyond his reach — even if he could somehow break down the barrier that being a transient lawman imposed.

Thirteen

—"Just keep your danged shirt on — they'll be coming," Fontana said irritably. He threw a glance to the eastern horizon. It was cold and he'd be mighty glad when sunrise got there.

Charlie Durbin and Gabe Malick, both hunched against the eroded side of a low butte, stirred uncomfortably. Red had forbade building a fire to ward off the chill, claiming that Rye just might spot the smoke and thus the ambush would be spoiled.

Charlie said, "I'm beginning to think we're just horsing ourselves, trying to cut down that bastard. He's either too damned smart for us or else he's one of them lucky kind that can't nobody kill."

Fontana's derisive laugh was short, heavy with scorn. "Now, just where'd you ever run across a jasper that couldn't nobody kill?"

Durbin hawked, spat into the dust. "Well, I just can't put my finger on —"

"You're damn right you can't!" Fontana snapped. "There ain't no such a thing as having a charmed life — or whatever it's called. Goes for the marshal, too. He pulls on his pants same way as you do — one leg at a time — and a bullet'll put him in the boneyard just as quick as it will you or anybody else. All it takes is the guts to throw down on him and pull the trigger — which I ain't so sure you got, Charlie."

Durbin spat again, scrubbed at his mouth with the back of a hand. He flicked the redhead with a glance of disgust.

"Now, you know for damn sure the reason I — and Gabe here, too — didn't do no good back there was on account of the marshal's horse, prancing and jumping around right in front of him. Ain't that right, Gabe?"

"Sure is," Malick said grumpily.

"We never did get no good shot,"

Durbin continued. "You can't go blaming us for that."

"Maybe," Fontana said, "but I recollect seeing you standing right there close to me, your rifle up and pointing at Rye the same time I let go at him. Now, I'd like to know why you didn't pull your trigger? Maybe your bullet might've had better luck hitting him than mine did. Your chance at him was good as mine."

Charlie looked down, wagged his head, admitting his failure. "I don't know, Red — I just can't answer that. Maybe it's on account of Rye being a lawman, and shooting down a lawman —"

Fontana cursed. "Just what I'm talking about! You ain't got the guts!"

The outlaw swiped at the drops hanging from the tip of his nose, looked again to the east. The pearl flare was brightening and streaks of color were beginning to break through.

"Wondering about you, too, Gabe," Red continued, transferring his attention to the big man. "Why didn't you start shooting right off the bat? You had the same chance as me, too."

"The hell I did!" Malick declared. "I

136

was trying to get in closer —"

"So's you could spot that woman, see where she was. You sure didn't want to hit her!"

"No, sir, I sure didn't," Malick said blandly. "Anyways, we got some lead into him."

"*I* did you mean," Fontana corrected.

"All right, you did. It'll slow him down plenty, and he ain't going to be such a stem-winder when we go at him this time."

Fontana snorted. "You don't know that jasper much. Right now he'll be twice as dangerous as he was the first time — and you can figure on it!"

Red Fontana's whiskery features had hardened, become a flushed, set mask. His eyes burned with the fierceness of the hate he felt for the lawman, and as he spoke, the knuckles of the hand gripping his rifle turned white.

Malick had turned, was studying the man closely. Finally he said, "We'll nail him this time, Red, don't fret none about it. Me and Charlie'll be backing you right up to the last bullet."

"Unless you'd as soon we'd pull out and let you rustle up somebody else to help," Durbin said, a slightly hopeful note in his voice.

Fontana swore again savagely. "Now, just where in the hell could I get somebody to side me before Rye and them hayshakers show up? When're you going to start using your head?"

Durbin dropped his head again, once more stared at the ground between his booted feet. Malick glanced at him and then at Fontana.

"Aw, hell, Red, get off his back," he said. "Mine, too. We're here backing your play, ain't we?"

"For sure," Durbin added, taking heart. "And you ain't wanting to see that marshal dead any more'n I do — you know that. I got plenty of reasons to leave him somewhere along the trail for the buzzards and the coyotes — but I just ain't so sure it can be done."

"Why?" Fontana shouted, suddenly furious. "Why, for hell sake? You can't be a growed man and believe in this here charmed life thing!"

"I ain't sure no more what I believe in; but I know for dang sure that every time there's been somebody set out to get him, something always happens to mess it up, just like yesterday morning when you had him in your sights — me and Gabe, too — and then that horse of his'n kept standing in front of him so's none of us could get a clean shot! That's what I mean — something always turns up to save his hide."

"That ain't nothing but pure luck —"

"Maybe it is. What I'm telling you is that it always works for him — not for them that's out to do the killing. And what's more, seems they're always the ones who end up deader'n a doornail."

Gabe Malick nodded slowly. "Charlie's right. I recollect hearing of a couple of times when some boys laid for this here Doomsday Marshal. Was them folks had to bury — not him."

"You want to back off?" Fontana demanded, angry again. The sun was now breaking over the horizon and a warm light was spreading across the flats and the low hills. "If'n you do, say so, so's I can make my plans without you."

"Hell, Red, I ain't wanting to back out," Malick said, coming to his feet and leaning against the butte.

"Me, neither," Durbin said, "but planning's what we need. We was going to have us a plan yesterday morning, only we didn't. Maybe this time if you'll work everything out ahead of time, we'll get the job done."

"This time we're going to," Fontana stated flatly.

Malick nodded. "Good, let's hear it. I'm wanting to get this here shindig over with 'cause I got some other plans for myself."

"Then do some listening," Red said, leaning forward, elbows on his knees. "We're going to split up. We know Rye and them pilgrims'll be coming down the Trail so we can be waiting for them in them rocks and brush back up the ways a piece —"

"Was what we tried doing yesterday," Malick said. "Didn't work out so good."

"Was because we didn't split up like I was wanting us to. We was all standing there in a bunch."

Durbin nodded. "Yeh, come to think of it, we was. Guess we just didn't get all set before the marshal come along."

"Ain't exactly it," Fontana said, "but it's sort of the idea. One thing, however, you birds ain't taking the job serious enough! You've got it in your heads that bushwhacking him'll be a cinch."

"I'm taking it plenty serious," Charlie muttered.

Malick grinned, slapped Durbin on the back. "You're sure right there, Charlie! You took it so serious that you got yourself a case of buck fever — or maybe we best call it marshal fever, when you lined up on Rye."

Durbin refused to be angered. Reaching down he picked up a handful of gravel, began tossing the pebbles at a large rock a few yards away. After a time he shrugged.

"Hell, I ain't ashamed of it — and Red there knows I've pulled the trigger on a man before — three, in fact, so it's not that I'm against killing, it's just that shooting down a lawman, specially this one's, different."

"No it ain't," Fontana said flatly. "It's you telling yourself it is and making yourself believe it."

The sun was well started on its climb now and the warmness was beginning to be felt. Loosening his brush jacket, Malick dug the makings from his shirt pocket, began to roll a cigarette.

"We better be getting down to

business and quit hashing yesterday over," he said. "Rye'll be showing up pretty soon. What's this here plan you got all schemed out for us to go by?"

Fontana bobbed his head. "It's this," he said crisply. "Two of us — me and Charlie, I reckon — will move up into them rocks I was talking about, only one of us'll be high up on the slope, other'n'll be down low.

"Gabe, I want you to ride on a ways, get maybe fifty, sixty yards ahead of us. When Rye and them hayshakers comes along, you'll let them go on by, hold off until they're about halfways between us, then we'll all open up. Me and Charlie'll be hitting Rye from the front and you'll be coming at him from the back. You savvy — both of you?"

Charlie nodded. Gabe said, "Sure ought to work. We'll have him trapped in a cross fire."

"Just what I'm wanting," Fontana said. "Now, what I don't want is some pussyfooting around. When I cut loose on him that'll be the signal for you two to open up — and I want you to keep pouring lead down there at him till your gun's empty. You got that, too?"

Both men signified that they under-
stood. Fontana spat, grunted in
satisfaction. "All right then, let's move
out and get set. You just follow me."

Leading his horse, Red Fontana
headed off across the slope. Durbin,
taking up the reins of his horse, fell in
behind him and was quickly followed by
Malick.

"While we're doing some talking, I got
me a little bit to say," Gabe stated as
they progressed slowly over the unstable
surface of the grade.

"Yeh?" Fontana answered.

"When you and Charlie start doing all
that shooting, I'm warning you again to
be careful and not hit the woman."

Fontana laughed. "Sure, Gabe, sure.
We'll be real careful, won't we,
Charlie?"

"Reckon so," Durbin said. "Did you
get a good look at her, Gabe?"

"Some —"

"She a young or a old woman?"

"Young. Couldn't tell too much — her
a'wearing an old pair of pants and a shirt
like she was — but she looks mighty good
to me."

"You for sure going to grab her and

take her back to your shack when the shooting's over?"

"Just what I aim to do."

"Means you'll have to plug that husband of hers, too, get him out of the way."

"So? What's one more killing? If they ever catch me, they can't hang me but once."

Fourteen

Morning found John Rye impatient and anxious to get under way. His arm was stiff after a night on his blanket and its paining did little to improve his mood. He was losing too much time, he felt, and with each passing hour was falling farther behind the killer who, he was now certain, was not one of the outlaw gang. The man, even if traveling at a leisurely pace, and assuming he had not turned off or doubled back, would soon out-distance him unless he could somehow speed things up.

Hurriedly saddling and bridling his horse, Rye quickly tied his blanket roll and other gear in place and turned to assist Ben Chase, making ready his and

Patience's horses.

"Mite cold this morning," the homesteader said cheerfully, and then, as Rye began to work on the woman's mount, added: "Ain't no cause for you to do that, Marshal. Time Patience gets the vittles together, I'll have them both fixed to go."

"I want to move out as soon as possible," Rye said in his clipped way. "Maybe you can give your wife a hand, help hurry things along there while I look after the horses."

Ben half turned, glanced at Patience. "Ain't no point — she's doing the best she can, and I'd only be in the way. Takes just so much time to make water boil and meat to cook. . . . Is it that killer you're chasing that's fretting you?"

The lawman continued to work. Shortly he said, "I'm falling too far behind. I'm afraid I'll lose him at the rate I'm going."

"Which is on account of being slowed down by me and Patience," Ben said. "If we wasn't along, hanging onto your coattails, you'd maybe've caught up with him by now."

"Possible, but you can't be blamed for those damned outlaws dogging me, or for the bullet I took in my arm. That would have happened whether you were along or not."

"Yeh, guess so, but I'm thinking it'd be better for you to go on without us. We can make it all right now — and we're bound to be coming to a big town pretty soon."

Nothing would suit him better, Rye thought. Alone he could travel fast, make up a few of the miles that he'd lost. Sure, there'd be the three outlaws to be on the watch for, and riding hard wouldn't do his arm any good — like as not start it to bleeding badly again and cause him considerable trouble — but he reckoned he could stand it. He'd been hurt before and had managed to get by; and catching Orson Brite's killer was of such importance that it called for going all out to bring the man down.

But there was Patience to be considered. Rye looked over his shoulder at the woman. He had avoided her as much as possible that morning hoping to spare her any embarrassment she might feel after the incident of the previous night.

She was standing near the fire, a long wire fork in one hand with which she had been stirring the meat in the spider. A wisp of hair had come down and was brushing against her face and her eyes appeared red — from the smoke, he hoped. Evidently she had heard what Ben said, was now watching Rye, waiting for his reply. When he caught her glance she did not turn away but, almost defiantly, continued to wait.

"I don't figure that'd be smart," he said, resuming work on the horse. "Expect I'd better stick with you until we reach some place where you and your wife will be safe." He could do that much for Patience.

"Maybe take a couple, three days."

Rye shook his head. "Doubt that. We're getting close to the crossroad that runs to Denver — we have to be, judging by the distance we've come. There's certain to be a town there."

"But if we're that close to the cross-road, ain't that killer you're chasing apt to turn onto it and make a beeline for Denver? And a town big as they say it is, a man could sure hide out good."

"Expect you're right," the lawman

agreed.

He hoped that wasn't the way it would turn out. Not only was Denver large, as towns in that part of the country went, but he would have nothing to go on insofar as carrying out a search was concerned; he had no good idea of what the outlaw would look like for certain, what kind of horse he was riding, or any other detail that would help. His one lead would be that a rider had entered the town sometime within the past couple of days — and doubtless many riders would have done that.

Each time he thought it over, it boiled down to one practical answer: he needed to hurry, overtake Orson Brite's killer before he reached the crossroad and could turn west for the Colorado capital, or east to Kansas.

The marshal cast another side look at Patience. She was again busy at preparing the morning meal. It was evidently near ready as she had removed the pot of coffee from the fire and was setting out plates and cups for their use.

"Well, I sure hate putting you out," Ben said, finished with his horse and stepping back.

A hard grin split the lawman's lips. *If it wasn't for your wife, mister, I would've left you on your own that first morning!* he felt inclined to say, but he knew Patience would hear — and perhaps get the wrong idea as to his reason.

"All a part of wearing a star," he said and, pulling the saddle cinch tight about the horse, secured it and tucked the loose end of the strap into the ring. The job now done, he looked again to the woman.

His words and the urgency of his manner had not been lost on her. She had filled their plates with food, was pouring coffee into the cups.

"You can eat now," she called, and immediately began to store away the unused supplies in their proper sacks.

Rye, with Ben at his side, crossed to the fire. As he hunched, took up his plate, his eyes again met those of the woman. This time she turned away and, with her own plate in hand, began to eat.

Nearby blue-feathered camp robbers were fluttering about in the cedars, unaccountably aware that soon there would be scraps of food to be plucked from the dry needles and leaves and loose dirt.

Patience was finished with her meal within only minutes, and, topping it off with a cup of the chicory, she began to assemble and hastily clean the pans and other utensils used to prepare the meal.

Rye waited a few moments for Ben to speak out but when he did not, he said, "I'll help you with those soon's I've finished —"

"I can do it," she replied coolly and went steadily about the task.

By the time the lawman and Chase were through, only minutes later, Patience had everything collected but their plates and cups and the forks they were using. Adding them to the sacks, she took the reins of her horse and led the animal into the clearing.

"I'm ready when you are," she declared, affixing the flour sacks to her saddle. There was an edge to her voice.

The lawman considered her quietly. She returned his gaze and, with a slight toss of her head, said: "You are in a hurry, Marshal — I know that. I won't be the one to hold you back any more than is necessary."

The lawman shrugged, started for his

horse. "I'm obliged," he said. "I'll be only a moment."

She was mounted and waiting by the time he and Ben had swung up onto their horses and had drawn alongside. When the lawman's glance met hers she smiled, as if cherishing her small victory. Rye grinned his acknowledgment, and looked off down the Trail.

"Can expect those outlaws to be somewhere ahead," he said.

"If they ain't gone and quit," Ben commented arbitrarily.

Rye, patient, said: "Like to think so but we can't bank on it. Best we all keep a sharp lookout. I'll stay in the lead, you two keep back of me a bit. If something starts I want you to run for the brush — or whatever cover's handy."

"How about your arm, Marshal?" Patience asked, her words still somewhat precise and businesslike. "The dressing hasn't been changed."

"It'll do," the lawman said. "You understand what I said?"

"Sure do, Marshal," Ben assured him. "If there's any shooting we're to hightail it into the brush. Now, if you want I'll take my gun, pitch in — help —"

The offer came as somewhat a surprise to the lawman. He shook his head. "No, it'll be better if you look out for your wife and yourself."

Saying no more, Rye roweled the chestnut gently and started the big horse forward. Patience and Ben swung in behind him a length or so, both looking back as the camp robbers, unable to restrain themselves any longer, rushed in, scolding noisily as they fought for the discarded scraps.

The sun was warm and Rye quickly removed his poncho and crammed it into one of his saddlebags. Shortly the Trail cut sharply down off the slope, began to follow a path that cut a course through a welter of rocks and brush in the bottom of the canyon. Haste was out of the question.

Swearing silently, Rye suppressed his need to hurry. He realized he could do nothing but allow the big gelding to pick his footing at his own pace. There was one consolation: the killer would have been faced with the same problem and compelled, likewise, to proceed with caution.

The heat continued to mount and

behind him Rye heard Ben's remarks concerning such as he removed his jacket. Patience made a reply of some sort but her voice was low and the lawman failed to catch her words.

He didn't like the country through which they were passing. The slopes to either side were close. Brush grew thick upon them and there were numerous boulders large enough for a man and a horse to hide behind. It was an ideal place for an ambush.

The thought redoubled John Rye's caution. He stirred on the saddle, raised himself in the stirrups, and had a long, probing look at their surroundings. What he saw only increased his dissatisfaction and convinced him the more that if the outlaws planned to attack again, undoubtedly this would be the place.

Twisting about, he glanced at the Chases. Patience was behind him no more than a stride away. Ben was a short distance back of her.

"Keep a close watch," he warned. "Don't think I've ever seen a better place for bushwhackers."

"Sure is a dandy, all right," the homesteader agreed. "Sure

getting warm."

The lawman pointed at the sky to the west. Heavy, dark clouds were scudding across the arch of blue and beginning to cover it over.

"Rain coming," he said.

"Ain't no doubt of that," Ben said. "Was I home I'd say there was a gully-washer on the way. Around here I don't know."

"Can't do much but guess myself," the lawman said. "Could be a bad one, though, if a man can go by those clouds. Look like they're plenty full of water."

"That's how I figure them, too —"

John Rye stirred wearily. Frustration was at last beginning to wear on him. They were moving all too slow as it was, and if a heavy rain or a cloudburst struck the canyon he might as well forget trying to overtake Brite's murderer before he reached the Denver crossroad; he'd have to start making altogether new plans.

But he'd face that problem if and when it came. "We get to that turn in the Trail where it's a bit wider," he said, pointing ahead, "we'll stop and you and your wife can put on your slickers."

"I ain't got one," the homesteader

said. "Patience ain't either. Reckon we'll just have to use our coats."

"Your wife can wear mine," Rye said. A coat would be of little or no protection at all, depending upon the severity of the storm. "I can put on my poncho."

They reached the bend, rounded it, and halted. The lawman turned about on his saddle, began to untie the blanket roll behind the cantle with which he carried his raincoat — paused, a warning suddenly racing through him.

Up on the slope to their left, metal had glinted in the driving sunlight. Abruptly tense, eyes fixed on the spot, Rye remained motionless. It came again — a tiny flash, and along with it slight movement deep within the pile of boulders.

"Off your horses!" he shouted, and threw himself from his horse.

Instantly rifle shots broke the pre-storm hush. The charged air became filled with their echoes and the shrill screaming of bullets ricocheting off close-by rocks.

Fifteen

Those damned outlaws again! The anger that swept John Rye as he hit the ground nullified the pain of the jarring impact. Rocking to one side, the lawman bounded to his feet and, pistol in hand, rushed for the brush at the foot of the slope.

He didn't halt there and, spurred by rage and frustration, he began a headlong climb for the spot where he'd seen the glint of metal. The bushwhackers' rifles — no target now in sight — had fallen silent, but the marshal had the general location firmly in mind, a large mound of boulders next to which was a stunted cedar tree.

He'd had enough. This time he

intended to put an end to the harassment he was taking from the outlaws, whoever the hell they were, once and for good. They had given him nothing but trouble — delays, a bullet wound in the arm, and, all in all, interfered with him doing his job. But this was where it was going to stop; he'd forget Orson Brite's murderer long enough to have it out with them, and then, assuming he survived, he could go on about his business.

Rye jerked back, ducked to one side. A figure had suddenly appeared — not at the pile of boulders toward which he was climbing — but lower on the slope and a short distance farther on. Instinctively Rye snapped a shot at the man. He saw him pull back quickly as the bullet missed, struck a rock nearby, and whined off into the darkening sky.

Immediately the rifleman behind the boulders opened up. Bullets began to slap into the loose dust and gravel, glance off the rocks above the lawman. The outlaw on below took up the barrage from his position and Rye, caught in a cross fire, dropped full length to the ground.

Pinned down, the lawman lay motionless with bullets hammering all about him. He could not continue to climb, he realized, nor could he back off; either way he would risk exposing himself to the outlaws. He could only wait.

After what seemed many minutes to him, the firing slowed, became spasmodic. Carefully then, he raised his head slightly for a better look at his surroundings. There was a chance, he saw, that by staying flat on his belly, he could worm his way backward, laterally across the slope to where a welter of rocks and brush formed a ragged knob. Reaching there he should be able to again start —

"Hey, Red, you reckon we got him?"

Red . . . The lawman gave the name consideration. The question had been directed to the outlaw hiding behind the large boulders near the top of the slope. Red — who? Rye raked his brain struggling to remember, to place the name, could not pin it down. Of course he had encountered many men with that nickname during his life, but could think of none who might be out to kill him.

"Ain't no telling. Keep watching."

Red's voice did have a vaguely familiar sound to it, but there was nothing definite enough to tie in with any memory. Regardless, he could not remain where he was. Eventually one of them would work himself around to where he would have a better view, and consequently a clear shot.

Besides, there was a third outlaw; where the hell was he? The question, suddenly presented to Rye by his consciousness, increased his urgency to move, to work his way out of the corner in which he found himself before the absent outlaw came at him — probably from an opposite side.

Taut, the lawman began to inch his way, feet-first, through the stubby weeds and loose gravel. The pain in his bandaged arm, unnoticed during those first flaring moments of excitement as he climbed up the slope, was now throbbing intensely, and he winced each time he was forced to put his weight on it. But he did not allow it to slow his progress, simply clamped his jaw and continued the agonizing process of retreating to the rocky knoll.

"Charlie — you see him yet?" Red called.

Charlie . . . It was another common

name that struck no familiar chord insofar as the lawman was concerned.

There was a minute's silence and then the man lower down on the slope replied. "Nope, ain't seen nothing. Getting the feeling we got him. Where you reckon Gabe is?"

"Hell — I don't know," Red's voice was filled with disgust.

Rye, not pausing, rolled the name of the third outlaw about in his mind. There was a Gabe Malick, he recalled, who had killed a man and then disappeared. He'd received a wanted poster on him — big, mean, and reported to be very dangerous. No one knew what had become of him, exactly, and no one outside of lawmen cared. A saloon girl-friend of his, asked casually in passing by Rye if she had seen the outlaw lately, had shaken her head and stated in no uncertain terms that she had not and hoped to the Almighty that she never would.

It could be Gabe Malick, and Rye could recall no reason why the big outlaw would have it in for him to the extent that he'd want to kill him — unless, of course, it was the simple fact of him being a lawman.

Rye felt his feet come up against the solid mass of rocks and brush toward which he was moving. Grunting in relief and satisfaction, and remaining tight to the uneven ground, he pivoted about to where he could have a close look at the mound.

He need only maintain a course to the right to get himself in behind the ragged pile. Once there, if his luck still held and his movements continued to go unnoticed by all of the outlaws, he could be safe.

Sweating freely, and his arm figuratively on fire, the lawman resumed his tedious advance, pausing every few moments to catch his breath, ease the pain, and throw a cautious glance in the directions where he knew two of the outlaws — Red and Charlie — were hiding. Gabe was something else. Rye had no idea where he might be and could only hope that he'd reach the shelter of the rocks and be ready when the man did show up.

Breathing hard, the lawman gained the far side of the pile, halted. For a full minute he lay there in the streaming sunlight, gathering himself, regaining his wind, and then abruptly, he sprang upright and dodged into the cluster of rocks.

Strangely, there was no instantaneous hail of lead from the bushwhackers. Either he had caught them all with attentions occupied elsewhere, or the mound by which he crouched was beyond their view.

Cool, thrusting aside his nagging pain, the lawman reloaded his pistol, thumbed a half-a-dozen or more cartridges from the loops of his gun belt to carry in his left hand for quick application, should such become necessary.

A hard, straight grin split his lips. The edge was his now. The outlaws were unaware of his position, actually were half convinced that he had been hit, was probably dead. Such shifted the advantage to him.

Removing his hat, and bent low, Rye moved out from behind the mound and began to climb, making his way slowly and quietly as possible through the weeds and rocks toward the man called Red. Shortly the marshal caught sight of the outlaw's horse standing near the large boulder. Red would be close by.

Halting, Rye turned his attention to Charlie, the man farther down the slope. There was no sign of him, nor was there any indication as to the whereabouts of Gabe. The hard, mirthless grin once more split his mouth; it was beginning to look as if he'd have Red all to himself, that it would be just the two of them — one against the other. Grim, he renewed the ascent.

He was soaked with sweat, and the pain in his arm had settled into a dull throbbing again punctuated now and then with a sharp stabbing when he carelessly allowed the member to brush against a rock or, stumbling, jarred it.

But he gave his discomfort no thought. He was closing in on one of the men that was out to kill him; taking care of Red, removing him from the picture, would make it easy to go after Charlie, down the slope, and that done, he'd have only Gabe to settle with. If —

"Red — coming up at you —"

The warning shout came from Charlie. Rye swore savagely. The outlaw had spotted him, and his hope to surprise was lost. Instinctively he dropped low as both men began to trigger their weapons, and once again bullets thudded and screamed about him as they sought his blood.

He was as good as dead if he remained there. Hunched, Rye lurched forward, began to run up the slope, throwing himself from side to side, pointing for a solitary, large boulder that offered refuge.

He saw movement higher up near the horse that he had spotted, snapped a quick shot at the outlaw — undoubtedly Red. Pivoting, he threw two bullets at the man on down the slope.

Suddenly he heard the clatter of iron on rock, whirled back around and glanced to Red. The outlaw, hunched low in the saddle, was rushing off through the brush and boulders.

The lawman steadied himself, fired at the blurred shape passing in and out of the brush and rocks. He tried again but the hammer clicked on a dead cartridge. Muttering impatiently, the lawman flipped open the weapon's loading gate, rodded out the empties, and thumbed in fresh shells.

Why had Red so abruptly mounted up and turned tail? There could be but one explanation — he'd been hit, Rye concluded; that quick snap shot he'd fired into the rocks when he'd seen motion had been a lucky one — it had scored. Weapon now ready, Rye, conscious of Charlie and the missing Gabe and accordingly cautious, hurried on up the steep grade; it was doubtful, but he just might get another shot at Red.

The lawman slowed as the sound of the outlaw below pulling out reached him. Charlie, like Red, was little more than a series of quick, blurred flashes as he raced through the rocks and brush for the Trail. He'd reach it fast, and be gone.

But Red was hurt and that made a difference. Coming about, Rye headed down-slope for his horse, taking the descent in long, plunging strides that doubled and redoubled the pain in his arm but brought him to the bottom in only brief moments.

Sucking for wind, legs aching from the strain, he checked his impetus, wheeled, and hurried toward the chestnut, standing off to one side of the Trail. The big gelding would have it all over the horses of Red and Charlie; he'd overtake them both quickly, being fresher and starting off on a more solid surface.

John Rye came to a halt. Ben Chase lay motionless not far beyond the gelding, at the edge of the wide place in the Trail. Tense, alert for danger, the lawman wheeled slowly, eyes searching for both Patience Chase and the outlaw Gabe. There was no sign of either.

And then, as if to solve the problem for him, a distant, frantic scream reached John Rye's ears and understanding came to him: Gabe — it could only have been he — had somehow overcome Ben Chase and was carrying off Patience.

Malick had been crouched behind a dense screen of bitterbrush above and a bit to the north of the bend in the Trail when Rye and the Chases moved by. His part, as outlined by Red Fontana, he recalled, was to remain there until the lawman and the pilgrims had passed, and then when Red opened up with his rifle, he was to ride down and come in behind Rye, thus trapping the marshal between them.

A lecherous man who craved the company of a woman constantly, his solitary confinement to a shack deep in the hills where he could evade the lawmen hunting for him was a time of pure hell. Thus, when Rye and the Chases crossed below him his mind had instantly discarded Fontana's instructions and centered instead on the woman.

"A hell of a looker!" he muttered, nervously brushing at his mouth.

At the time Fontana, with Charlie Durbin in tow, had come to his hiding place in the hills and told him about his scheme to kill Marshal John Rye, he had agreed to participate. It was not so much for the joy and pleasure of ridding his kind of a lawman, but with the hope that he might find it safe to stop at one of the settlements they would be passing, visit one of the saloons, and satisfy his lust.

This would be a hundred times better than he'd hoped for! He'd not have to risk being recognized by some two-bit sheriff or deputy in some lousy, stinking town where people were always in such a hurry to use a rope on a man! No, sir — it was far from that! Luck was just handing him a prize right where he was!

And what a prize! A young woman, a real looker, and soon as Red and Charlie

168

got the marshal out of the way, and he took care of the pilgrim — a sodbuster judging from the clothes he wore — she'd be all his. He'd not fool around and waste time going on with Red and Charlie — he'd just snatch up his prize and light out for his shack.

A rifle shot echoed along the slope. That would be Red cutting down on the marshal. As other reports sounded, Gabe rose, swung up onto the saddle, and started down the grade. Below he saw that Rye and the pilgrims had come off their horses — evidently Red and Charlie had missed again — and the lawman was running toward the slope.

The hell with them. There was two of them — they could take care of Rye. He had plans of his own — plans that meant he'd have himself a mighty pretty little gal around the shack for as long as he wanted.

Malick reached the bottom of the grade in a cloud of thin dust, his horse pushing loose ground, dry weeds and other litter before him as his hoofs dug deep into the slope to keep from sliding.

Drawing his pistol, the outlaw jammed spurs into the flanks of his mount and, cutting the animal about, sent him charging straight for the homesteader and his woman. Both wheeled, surprise and fear on their faces.

Drawing close, Gabe abruptly veered his horse at the sodbuster, intending to run him down. The animal refused, swerved to avoid the collision. Malick leaned far over, swung the pistol clutched in his big hand, and, as the horse raced by, struck the pilgrim a solid blow on the side of the head.

He did not look around to see if the man went down — he knew full well that he would — and as the woman screamed, he pivoted his horse sharply, bringing it to its back legs as he did, and bore down on her. With the steady hammer of Red and Charlie Durbin's rifles filling the hot, dusty air, he rode in close. Pausing only for an instant, he reached down, caught the woman by her slim waist, and swept her off the ground.

She screamed again, began to struggle. Malick only grinned, and sliding her over the cantle, laid her across the seat of his saddle as he might a sack of grain, and rode on.

The jolting of the horse robbed her of

her breath, quieted her, and after a time Malick pulled to a halt. Taking her by an arm he turned her over, lifted her clear off the saddle and sat her on the hull as she should be. In that moment she screamed once more, a long, piercing sound that echoed across the low hills and flats and sent anger surging through Gabe Malick.

"You shut up!" he shouted, and cuffed her hard on the side of the head. "You yell again and I'll fix you good!"

Sixteen

Rye, all thoughts of going after Red and Charlie abandoned, hurried to Ben Chase's side and knelt beside him. The homesteader wasn't dead. He had been knocked unconscious by a blow to the head, receiving it undoubtedly when he tried to stop the outlaw from kidnapping his wife. He'd be all right.

Rising, the lawman returned to his horse and swung up onto the saddle. He dare not let Gabe get too far ahead, lest he lose him and Patience in the welter of brush and rocks. Cutting the chestnut about, Rye started back up the Trail. He couldn't be absolutely sure that the outlaw was taking the same course, but, logically, he would be; having left Ben dead, or at least unconscious, and in the belief that Red and Charlie had taken care of Rye, the man would not be worrying about any pursuit.

A rabbit shot out of the brush, crossed the path in front of the chestnut with a rapid flirting of its cotton white tail. The big horse veered sharply in stride, and loped on. He'd best get off the Trail, Rye realized, travel where the gelding's hoofs would make less noise. He'd do that shortly — at the first opportunity since he must be drawing close to the outlaw and the girl.

He hoped he could overtake them quickly. The delays he was encountering were making it easy for Judge Brite's murderer to escape — and that was going to be a hard fact to admit. John Rye prided himself on never losing a prisoner or failing to track down the man he was sent to get. This could be the time the latter part of his proud record would be broken.

But the hell with the record! The hell with Brite's killer and his going scot free! Patience Chase was more important than either at the moment, and if it took the rest of the day, or longer, to get her out of Gabe Malick's hands, so be it.

Rye grinned wryly at the vehemence of his thoughts. He had changed, he reckoned, or was changing. A situation such as this, concerning a woman, wouldn't have appeared so important a few years earlier. He would have accepted it, certainly, and assessed it as a duty, but it would have been in a more matter-of-fact manner, and he would not have permitted himself to become personally involved.

But then it wouldn't have been Patience Chase he was setting out to rescue — Patience, a beautiful young woman who had all but declared her love for him — despite her being the wife of another man. It had hurt to turn his back on her, chill her feelings for him, but he had no choice; there was no place in his way of life for a wife, and, under no circumstances would he be a party to breaking up a marriage.

He owed it to Patience to help her, and while he'd probably never lay eyes on her again once they reached a settlement where she and Ben would be safe, he'd always have the memory of her and the knowledge that he'd done all he could for her.

Rye drew up sharply. Far ahead, on a level stretch of trail, he saw a horse and rider — two riders. It was Gabe and Patience.

Immediately the lawman pulled farther away from the Trail. The canyon was somewhat narrow in that immediate area, but on a distance he could see that it widened considerably. Biding his time until he reached that point, Rye then increased the gelding's pace and, swinging wide, started a long curve that would eventually bring him out in front of the outlaw and his prisoner.

He began to think ahead, to consider the coming confrontation. Gabe Malick — and he was certain that it was Malick — was a dangerous, coldblooded killer. He would need to go at the man with care in order to avoid getting Patience hurt. He could expect it to be a touchy bit of work, and a great deal would depend on the woman's courage and presence of mind.

Shortly Rye found himself abreast of the couple, with much brush, rocks, and small trees screening him from their eyes. He hurried on and, when he reached what he believed was a safe margin, cut the gelding left and after a time reached the Trail. There, in a deep stand of scrub oak and other rank growth, he halted. Dismounting, Rye secured his horse and, gun in hand, crossed to a point where, unseen, he would have a clear view of the path.

Motionless, idly listening to a flicker tattooing a nearby tree, the lawman waited. Malick was not long in coming. In only moments the slow thud of a horse's hoofs on the hard surface of the Trail came to him. At almost the same instant he heard Patience cry out in pain, and then the deep-throated laugh of the outlaw. Words were then said but the marshal could not distinguish them, catching only the sound of Gabe's voice.

Abruptly Rye stepped out into the center of the path. The head of the outlaw's horse flung up as, startled, he checked his slow stride. Gabe's mouth sagged in surprise, and, jerking his arm from about Patience's waist, he made a stab for the pistol on his hip.

In that fragment of time Patience threw herself from the saddle to the ground. Rye's gun came up fast but the outlaw, seizing the opportunity, wheeled his horse broadside, dropped from the animal's back onto the woman. Seizing her by an arm, he dragged her upright and, using her as a shield, crouched behind her. Leveling his weapon at the lawman, he laughed.

"Now, Marshal, let's me and you do some shooting," he said. "Figured Red and Charlie took care of you, but I reckon they messed it up again. Leaves it to me."

"Turn the lady loose," Rye said coldly, uncompromisingly. It was Gabe Malick, all right; he recognized the outlaw from the poster he'd seen. "You'll only get her hurt —"

"I ain't about to turn her loose — no, sir! She's mine and I'm taking her back to my shack."

"You'll never make it, Gabe. I'm warning you now. I'll kill you whichever way you go — either through her or when you let her go. Your number's up."

"You know me, eh?" Malick said, pleased. "Then you know I ain't one to do no listening. Now, if you —"

"I'm not here to talk, either," the lawman cut in. "Are you going to take your hands off the lady or —"

Patience screamed abruptly. Doubling forward, she twisted free of the outlaw's grasp and threw herself to the ground.

Rye reacted instantly to the opportunity the woman had provided. His weapon roared as he triggered it. Gabe staggered back, a frown pulling at his dark, whiskered features. The gun in his hand discharged as reflexes set it off, the bullet harmlessly burying itself in the packed soil at his feet, and then, buckling, he went down.

Patience was on her feet and running to Rye in the succeeding moment. She reached him, threw her arms about his neck and, burying her face in his chest, began to sob.

"Oh, John — I was so scared! That man — that horrible animal, he —"

Jaw set, the lawman stood rigid, unbending, pistol in one hand, the other hanging loosely at his side.

"Nothing to worry about. He can't bother you now — not ever again."

Patience drew back from him slowly as if only then aware of his unrelenting coolness. Face tipped down, she produced a handkerchief, dabbed at her eyes. Looking up squarely at him, she managed a smile.

"I thought you had been killed. He kept telling me that. When you stepped out from behind that bush it was like — like a glimpse into heaven!"

"Didn't you figure your husband would be coming after you?" Rye asked, reloading his pistol.

"Well, yes, but I didn't know how bad he was hurt. That man — Gabe — tried to ride him down, and when he couldn't, he hit Ben with his pistol. Is he all right?"

"Expect so," the lawman said, holstering the weapon and, moving away from her, crossed to where Malick lay. He examined the outlaw briefly, assured himself that he was dead, and turned then to look for the man's horse. It had trotted off a distance from the Trail when the shooting erupted, would not require too much time and trouble to retrieve.

"We best get back to your husband," Rye said, wheeling to face the woman as a sense of urgency again began to hammer at him. "We'll have to ride double."

Patience met his direct gaze, nodded

soberly and followed him to where the chestnut was tied. Silent, she waited until he had mounted, and then accepting his extended hand, allowed him to swing her up to a place behind him on the saddle.

Equally wordless, Rye reined the gelding onto the path and headed back for the bend in the Trail where they had left Chase.

Seventeen

They reached the turn, rounded it, and stopped. Ben Chase was standing on the shoulder of the path, rubbing his head numbly. Hearing the thud of Rye's oncoming horse, he had turned, was facing toward his wife and the lawman as they pulled up.

Immediately Patience slid to the ground and rushed to Ben, her features strained and filled with anxiety.

"Are you bad hurt?" she asked.

The homesteader shrugged off the question. "What about you? Last I see was that bushwhacker riding straight at me."

"I'm all right — thanks to the Marshal," the woman replied. "I want

181

you to sit down there on that rock and let me have a look at that place on your head where you got hit. It's bleeding."

"Ain't hurting none," Ben said, mildly protesting, but he followed his wife's instructions.

Rye, still mounted, moved off to round up the two horses the Chases were riding, both having wandered off a short distance in search of grass. When he returned with them Ben was yet on the rock, but now with a strip of white cloth encircling his head. Since all supplies had been on the horses, Rye guessed Patience had improvised a bandage, using a piece of cloth no doubt ripped from one of the garments she was wearing. Such indicated that Ben's wound was of no consequence.

"Patience told me what you done for her," the homesteader said as the lawman halted and came off the saddle. "Sure am obliged to you."

The marshal nodded. He was again feeling the urge to hurry on, try to make up for lost time, but Chase's bland words brought his mind to a standstill. Ben had taken the kidnapping and the rescue of his wife in a most indifferent manner, it seemed to Rye. Most men, being unable to pursue on their own, would have been torn by worry, and, when reunited, shown great joy and relief.

As far as he knew Patience had been the only one to exhibit concern to any degree — and that was for the rap the homesteader had taken on the head. Their marriage, Rye was beginning to think, was a very casual and impersonal arrangement.

"Marshal, I want to change the dressing on your arm before we go on," Patience said. She was standing just beyond Ben, medical supplies taken from the saddlebags and now in her hands. "I'd better put some of Mama's salve on that cut on your head, too," she added, nodding to Ben.

Rye had glanced to the sun. It was well up and on its way across the sky, steadily filling with dark, threatening clouds drifting in from the west. Encountering the outlaws had cost him a good two hours, he reckoned.

"Let it go till we stop to eat," he said.

Patience, applying ointment to her husband's wound and restoring the bandage, shook her head. "No, we'd better not wait. It's started bleeding again — probably happened when you jumped from your horse and went up the slope after those outlaws. And there's dirt on the bandage. Probably in the wound, too. If I don't take care of it now there's a good chance it'll mortify."

The lawman gave that thought. He shrugged resignedly and, crossing to the rock vacated by Ben Chase, sat down. Anger was gripping him, directed not at the Chases particularly but at Red and Charlie and Gabe Malick, who were responsible for the delays which, in turn, represented failure on his own part. He could not recall ever experiencing as much frustration as he was encountering in the pursuit of Judge Orson Brite's murderer.

"This would have been almost healed if you hadn't torn it open," Patience said.

"Had to make a choice," Rye said dryly. "Was either jump off my horse — or get shot off."

"Of course," the woman said quickly. "I didn't mean that the way it sounded."

Off to the north of them in the brush and trees a cock grouse was drumming noisily, but elsewhere around them the birds and the usual insect chorus were silent as a stillness held the land.

The lawman glanced again to the sky. The clouds were now beginning to merge, darken with full bellies, and form an overcast. Rain was not far off — which would bring relief from the close heat but, conversely, hinder their progress.

He became aware that Patience had paused, Mason jar of salve in one hand, a folded bit of bandage in the other.

"Something bothering you?" he asked, impatient with her hesitation.

"Those men — the outlaws," she said with a shudder, "they intended to kill you and Ben and then — then take me off somewhere —"

"That was the way Gabe figured. I doubt if Red or Charlie were in on that."

"But they were the ones who started the shooting this morning —"

"I'm not saying they're not out to cut me down — for some reason I don't savvy. That's been the deal from the start. Gabe went after you on his own, I expect, and your husband got hurt when he got in the way."

Patience resumed her work, applying the ointment-coated pad to the now-clean wound and wrapping the arm with a new strip of white cloth.

"Do you know who they are now?" the woman asked, finishing. "You mentioned their names —"

"I heard the two up on the slope yelling back and forth. One's called Red, the other Charlie. Means nothing to me — I've run across a lot of Reds and Charlies in my life."

"But Gabe Malick — you seemed to know him."

"Never seen him in person until today," the lawman said, rising. "Did get a poster on him a while back. Was wanted for murder — killed a man over a woman, I think it said. He'd busted jail and gone into the hills to hide. When I saw him he fit the description that was on the dodger."

Patience, gathering up her medical supplies, paused, glanced off into the direction where the grouse was still busily drumming.

"His shack is a couple of days' ride from here, he said. Kept telling me about it, how we'd live there and nobody'd ever bother us because only a few of his friends knew where it was." A tremor again shook the woman. "Some of the things he said —"

"Best you forget him and what he said," Rye advised, "or at least try. He's where he'll never bother you or anyone else again." Pivoting, the lawman put his attention on Ben. "Any reason why you can't travel?"

Chase had found another place to sit, a grass hummock. He nodded slowly, got to his feet.

"I'm ready anytime."

Rye immediately crossed to where he had tethered the horses, side by side, to a cedar. Removing his slicker, he handed it to Patience, who had followed and was restoring the bandage cloth and jar of salve to their places.

"Rain'll be here soon," he said. "Best you put this on now."

She frowned, took the long, stiff garment from him. "Thank you — but what will you wear?"

"My poncho'll be enough. Can always use my blanket."

"I don't think you should get that arm wet —"

"Clean water never hurt anybody, they say," Rye replied, and glanced to Ben. "You got something you can put on? Got a hunch this is going to be a bad storm."

Chase had come up, was standing beside his horse. Reaching up, he began to untie the blanket roll on his saddle.

"Use that piece of canvas you've been sleeping on," Patience suggested. "Can wear it like a shawl."

Chase said nothing. The roll released, he took the square of duck cloth the woman had mentioned from the remainder of his bedding and hung it on the horn. Restoring the blanket to the cantle, he draped the canvas about his shoulders and, mounting, looked down at Rye.

"You're wanting to hurry — I'm ready."

The lawman saw Patience flash a look of irritation at the homesteader, but he let the man's words pass and assisting the woman into the slicker helped her up onto the saddle. Lightning flashed suddenly, splitting the mass of lowering clouds and releasing a deep-throated roll of thunder that stilled even the amorous grouse.

Rye, dropping his poncho over his head, having removed it minutes earlier for Patience's convenience in caring for his wounded arm, settled it about his shoulders and swung up onto the chestnut.

At that moment the sky opened and the rain started, coming down at first in large, tentative drops, well spaced apart that sent up miniature geysers of dust when they met the dry earth, and filled the air with an odd suffocating smell. And then suddenly, as if the clouds had been tipped completely, it began to rain in earnest.

"We ain't going to get far in this," Ben said, having to raise his voice to be heard above the hammering drops. "You reckon we better hole up around here somewhere until it stops?"

The marshal glanced about. "You see anyplace where we could go to get out of it? Nothing here but open country."

The homesteader shrugged. He was holding the bit of canvas over his head like an umbrella, endeavoring to keep the rain off, and was succeeding fairly well.

"No, reckon not —"

"Then we're just as well off riding on — can't get any wetter," Rye said and, raking the chestnut with his spurs, led off down the Trail. They'd not be traveling at any speed, he realized, but there was some satisfaction in knowing that they at least were moving — and every mile put behind them was one more they'd not have to cover in the days to come.

The rain lasted off and on the entire day. Several times the horses slipped on the wet clay, but none sustained any injury — nor did the lawman and the Chases, all of whom were able to jump free and avoid being caught under the thrashing animals. When they finally halted in a grove of trees for the night, only Patience was not soaked to the skin and covered with mud.

Rye thought little of it. Discomfort on the trail was not new to him, and shortly after they had pulled up he turned the horses over to Ben and began to search about in the debris accumulated under the trees for dry wood. Collecting an armload, he returned to camp where Patience, selecting a place away from the dripping boughs, was setting out food and the utensils in which to prepare it, and he built a fire.

The heat felt good, and for a few moments he stood there beside it, letting the warmth of the flames penetrate his soggy clothing and reach his skin. Patience, nearby, glanced up at him.

"I'm sure you'll be glad when you can get us off your hands. We've done nothing but hold you back."

"The outlaws — and this rain — have had plenty to do with it. Can't blame it all on you folks."

"Perhaps, but if we hadn't been along —"

"It'll all work out," Rye said, his shoulders stirring. "Could be I've lost that killer by now — won't know until we come to the next town — but if I have I'll keep at it till I find him."

Patience nodded slowly, removed the lid from a Mason jar, and dumped the beans she had been soaking in water for several days into a kettle and set it over the flames.

"Yes, I'm sure you will," she murmured.

Eighteen

"Do you think we'll be bothered by those outlaws again?" Patience asked the next morning after they had gotten underway.

It had been a later start, to Rye's thinking, but it had been as much his fault as the Chases'. They had spent the first hour cleaning themselves up, which entailed mostly removing mud from their clothing and gear after allowing it to dry overnight. Rye took an extra few minutes to shave, having so far ignored the chore since Scott's Bluff, but he was never very faithful to what many men ritually observed daily, particularly while he was on the trail.

The lawman settled the still damp poncho about his shoulders. The rain had left the land well soaked and there was a coolness in the air despite the sun, already on its way.

"Anybody's guess," he said. "Could be they've had enough and aim to forget it now."

The path had climbed up onto a broad prairie dotted with bayonet yucca, occasional cedars, and low clumps of weeds. Traveling was easy, and Rye and the Chases were riding abreast beneath the spotlessly clean sky.

"Forget it?" Ben echoed. "It ain't likely. They're out to get you, Marshal. What makes you think they'll quit now?"

"I put a bullet into one of them back there on the slope — the man called Red. Can't say how bad hurt he was but he mounted up and rode off right after with his sidekick, Charlie, following. Was coming back down to get my horse and go after them when I found you down, knocked cold, and your wife gone."

Patience smiled. "You see, it was us again that got in your way and kept you from doing your job."

The lawman shook his head at her wry observation. "Might have caught up with them, and maybe not. They had a good start on me."

"Didn't know you'd plugged one of them," the homesteader said. "That'll make a difference, all right, same as there ain't but a couple of them now, Gabe being out of it. Him not showing up and joining them — you reckon they'll figure he's dead?"

"Probably," the lawman said.

"One thing for sure," Ben continued, "if they are hanging around, waiting, we'll sure see them from a long ways off. Ain't nothing but flats far as a man can see."

Rye agreed, but adhering to his rule of never taking anything for granted in such circumstances, he continued to maintain a sharp watch on the country not only ahead and to the sides, but behind them as well.

They rode on at last making good time. At noon the lawman called a halt in a hollow a short distance from the Trail to rest the horses and let them water from a pool gathered in the bottom of the swale. Patience came up with a quick lunch of dried meat, biscuits, and home-canned peaches. It was necessary to forego coffee as there was no wood, dry or otherwise, to be found.

Within an hour they were again in the saddle and moving southward steadily, and since they were traveling at such a good pace, the lawman began to feel better about trimming the lead the killer he was pursuing had on him and possibly even overtaking him before he reached the Denver-Kansas crossroad. The storm would have slowed him down also, and —

"Going to have to pull up —"

At Ben Chase's words, Rye swore silently. There was no end to delays, to trouble.

"Why?" he asked, voice tight.

"Horse is losing a shoe again."

The lawman, temper barely controlled, pulled the gelding to a halt. Patience drew in beside him.

"I thought you fixed that loose shoe back at Cow Springs —"

"Tried," the homesteader said, off the saddle and rapping his horse on the knee and inducing him to lift his leg so that the hoof could be examined. "Wasn't nothing much to work with and there wasn't nobody around to help me find what I needed."

Rye was staring ahead, hat tipped forward to shade his eyes as he studied the horizon beyond a band of brushy hills into which the plain was dissolving.

"There some way you can keep the shoe on for a few more miles?" he asked. "Can see smoke."

Patience, features lighting up at his words, turned quickly. "Is it the town we've been looking for?"

Rye agreed that she was probably right. They had covered what he believed was the necessary distance to arrive at the crossroad and, consequently, at the settlement he felt certain would be found there.

Ben, hands on hips, hawked, spat. "Reckon I can, Marshal," he said, replying to Rye's question, "but it'll take a while. Might be best if you'd go on. Me and Patience'll be all right now."

The lawman cast a side glance at the woman. Her gaze was fixed on the brush-covered hills they must yet pass through and he could see the apprehension in her eyes. That she did not agree with her husband and still feared trouble from the outlaws was evident. As to the latter, John Rye reckoned he could not blame

196

her; she'd had a terrifying experience with Gabe Malick and the dread of encountering another such as him again would likely remain with her for a long time.

"No need," he said. "The town can't be far, and another hour or so's not going to make all that much difference. Something I can do to help you?"

The homesteader glanced down at the horse's hoof, caught between his own knees. "I've got to set these nails again. Guess I'll have to use a rock for a hammer — that'n laying there near you'll do. Just you toss it to me and I'll get busy."

Rye dismounted, picked up the designated stone and, handing it to Chase, moved away. Patience, too, had left her saddle and, finding a slight rise in the land, was sitting there looking off in the direction of the smoke. She smiled at the lawman as he stopped beside her.

"I hope it's a town that amounts to something," she said wistfully. "I'm so tired of being nowhere, of seeing nothing but empty plains and brushy hills — and nobody but outlaws — men you have to be afraid of."

"Expect it'll be a fair-sized place. Probably several roads and trails meet there, and wherever that happens, there's always a good town. I'm hoping strong that it'll be on a regular stage line."

"Why?"

"I'd like to see you and your husband climb aboard a coach and take it all the way to Texas. I don't think you're fixed for traveling across country — and it'd be a lot safer."

The marshal, with a wealth of experience gained from traveling back and forth through the frontier, had been surprised at the Chases when he learned they were undertaking a journey of such length with no more equipment and supplies than he noted. He was unaware of the circumstances surrounding their decision to move, of course, but if a wagon was not available they surely could have provided a packhorse.

Patience waited while he settled on his heels and then, studying him closely, said: "Does that make a difference to you — our being safe?"

Rye's attention was back on the smoke. "Well, I sure wouldn't want something to happen to you — after all you've gone through getting this far.''

''I appreciate that, Marshal,'' the woman said quietly.

Ben was hammering industriously at securing the iron shoe to his horse's hoof, that racket stilling the insects in the weeds and stubby grass around them. The sky was still washed clean of clouds, and the sun, unlike the previous day, was enjoying an uncluttered path as it climbed across the blue arch.

It had grown much warmer since midday, and Rye, having shed his poncho, was now unbuttoning the front of his shirt. Patience, also, had loosened her clothing and was fanning herself with a bit of cloth as she continued to stare off into the distance.

''I don't suppose we'll ever meet again after we part in that town,'' she said, after a time.

The lawman's shoulders lifted, fell. ''Hard to say. Job takes me around the country considerable. Like as not I'll be through the part of Texas where your relatives live someday. Would drop by, say howdy, if I knew the name of the place.''

"I don't know what it's called," Patience replied. "And they aren't relatives — just a friend of Pa's."

Rye's thick brows drew together. "Thought he told me you'd be living with relations —"

"I think he did — but he wasn't telling the truth."

"Why would he lie to me about it? No reason —"

"I expect he was a little ashamed to admit that we had no place to go. Don't hold it against him, Marshal."

"Can't see as it makes any difference, one way or the other," the lawman said, but it always disturbed him to find that he'd been lied to, and he was wondering if there was another reason why the homesteader had not told him the truth. But as he'd said — it didn't matter.

A half hour later they were again on their horses and moving toward the distant settlement, slowly to be sure because of the temporary nature of the repair Ben had made, but progressing, nevertheless.

Near the middle of the afternoon they broke out of the brushy hills, having passed through them without incident, and dropped into a broad, shallow valley in which a surprisingly large town lay. The area was green with grass and shaded by many trees, and the small, outlying farms, nurtured by a sparkling creek that ran lengthwise through the settlement, appeared healthy and prosperous.

From their slightly higher position on the Trail at the edge of the valley, they could see numerous homes standing along the several streets, and the center of town, a cluster of one- and two-storied, false-fronted buildings, provided the intersection point for the two main roads that could be seen running to all four directions.

Rye, studying it all closely as they approached, heard Patience sigh with relief, grateful they had at last reached the place of civilization that she had been longing for.

His attention, however, now settled on the first structure that they would encounter as they entered the settlement — a broad, sprawling structure with numerous corrals and a sign on its facade bearing the words: BILLY GRINDLE LIVERY STABLE. Anyone coming in from the north on the Arapaho Trail would pass by the Grindle establishment, the lawman realized.

Saying nothing to the Chases, he headed directly for the place and drew up at the wide doors opening into its runway. At once a smiling, elderly man in clean overalls and black sateen shirt appeared.

"Howdy, folks, I'm Billy Grindle," he greeted. "I reckon you're wanting to stable your animals."

Rye nodded, said, "Need a bit of information first. Expect you see everybody that rides in off the Trail."

"Sure do — day and night!" Grindle replied. "Have to. Couple of other livery stables here in Alamo Butte and I've got to hustle to get my share of the business. Why you asking? You looking for somebody special?"

"Would've been a man rode in here on a bay horse — most likely alone — probably within the last couple of days. That's about all I can tell you about him."

Grindle pushed his fairly new straw hat to the back of his head, rubbed at his jaw. "Well, was a couple of riders showed up here this morning — early.

But a day or two ago, I don't recollect
— oh, yeh, I'm forgetting. Was someone
come in day before yesterday."

The lawman had come to attention, his
deep-set eyes fixed on the stable owner.
"You know which way he went when he
left town?"

"He didn't," Grindle replied flatly.
"Lives here. Name's Pearly — Dave
Pearly. Been visiting up Wyoming way,
I think."

John Rye gathered up his reins. Face
bleak, eyes seemingly receded deeper
into their shadowed pockets, he came
slowly about.

"You folks wait here for me," he said,
nodding to Ben and Patience, and then
put his attention once again on Grindle.
"Where'll I find this Dave Pearly?"

The livery stable man took a few steps
farther into the open and pointed toward
the center of town. A look of concern
crossed his features and he lowered his
arm.

"I ain't going to get Dave in no
trouble, am I, mister?" he asked.

"It's nothing you'll have any part of,"
the lawman replied. "Where will he be?"

Grindle again adjusted his hat and then

once more pointed toward town. "Keep going right on down the road till you come to a cross street — the first one. Turn left and go about a mile."

"Will it be a farm or a ranch — or just a home?"

"Reckon you could say it'd be a little bit of all three — but mostly it's where Dave lives. You can't miss it. Place has a rail fence around it that's just been whitewashed."

"Obliged to you," Rye said and, wheeling the chestnut about, moved off at a lope.

Nineteen

Dave Pearly's home, as Billy Grindle had said, was not difficult to find. It was simply a matter of going to the first cross street, turning left, and shortly there it was.

With his customary caution, Rye halted at the corner of the property, encircled by a two-railed, white fence, and studied the house, a small, wooden square with a pitched roof. It projected no personality whatsoever. But he was interested at that moment in locating its doors and windows, and in getting the general layout of the place.

He could see no one anywhere in the extensive yard or around the small barn at the rear of the lot. There was a yellow-wheeled buggy pulled up, with shafts suspended, beneath an open-end shed, and he noted four horses in a back corral.

It didn't look to be the sort of place, so neat and orderly, where a man could expect to find a coldblooded killer residing. But John Rye had been around long enough to know there was no specific type, that you could never judge by appearances. Given sufficient cause and reason, he believed that any person could turn to murder.

Clucking to the gelding, the lawman rode on, following along the rail fence until he came to a swing gate. Remaining in the saddle, he leaned forward, lifted the loop of wire from the post, and as the octagonal barrier opened, passed through. Again halting, he closed the gate, secured it, and then, taut, eyes probing ceaselessly, and fully on the alert for any untoward movement anywhere around or within the house, he continued.

There was no hitch rack in front of the house and, leaving the chestnut standing in the shadow of a large apple tree, Rye stepped up to the door, rapped sharply, and stepped aside to wait. He had no way of knowing what the response to his knock would be and what he could expect. If Dave Pearly was the killer — and there seemed no doubt that he had just ridden down from Wyoming on the Arapaho Trail — and if Pearly recognized him as a lawman, there would be trouble.

No answer came to his summons. Rye knocked again, louder and more insistently, and once more, hand now resting on the butt of his pistol, drew back. And then from somewhere inside the house, a voice sounded.

"Coming! I'm coming!"

Rye stood motionless, ready. The door lock rattled, the panel opened, and a narrow, elderly face peered out.

"What do you want?"

"Dave Pearly," Rye said. "Like to talk to him."

"What about?"

"I'll tell him. He around somewhere?"

"I'm Pearly. What do you want?"

The lawman frowned. Brite's murderer was said to be young, probably strong, tall; but witnesses, even when close by and afforded a good look at a malefactor, often came up with conflicting and erroneous descriptions.

"You mind coming out here on the porch?" the lawman said.

Rye had placed the request more in the nature of a suggestion, but his tone left little doubt that he expected the man to comply.

Pearly shrugged, moved out into the open. He was unarmed, the lawman saw first, and then frowned again. Dave Pearly was actually below average stature, and far from young. He had graying hair and mustache, faded eyes, was a bit stoop-shouldered, and did not limp.

"Now I've done what you wanted — now you favor me," he said, his voice rising slightly in anger. "Who the hell are you and what do you want?"

"Name's Rye. I'm here to ask you a question or two."

"About what?"

"Did you ride in from the north on the Arapaho Trail a couple of days ago?"

"Yeh, sure did. What's that got to —"

"Coming from where?"

"Wyoming — Laramie. Dammit, Mister Rye, you ain't getting one more word out of me until you tell me —"

"I'm a U. S. Marshal — working on a killing."

"Killing!" Pearly echoed, his eyes widening. "Whose?"

Rye gave that a few moments' thought, said, "I'll lay it out for you after a bit. First I'd like to know what you were doing in Laramie."

"That where this killing took place?"

"No —"

Pearly's thin shoulders stirred. "Was burying my brother. Got word that he'd died from the undertaker, and him not having no kin but me, I had to make the trip up there and take care of it — him."

"Can you prove that?"

Dave Pearly spat into the dust at the end of the porch. "Do I need to?"

"Yes, you need to," Rye stated flatly. "Judge Orson Brite was shot to death in a town called Gellen, which is close to Laramie. Man who did it rode out and headed south on the Arapaho Trail. I've got two witnesses who heard a rider on the Trail at about the time the killer would be there."

"And you're trying to say it was me?"

"I'm going by what facts I've got. You rode in here two days ago. Backing the time up, that puts you right there."

Concern began to fill Pearly's eyes and tear at his lean features. "Hell, Marshal — a lot of folks use the Arapaho —"

"Just happens you and the two people I said heard you were the only travelers these last few days. There were three outlaws hanging around, but they're out of it far as Brite's murder is concerned."

Pearly brushed nervously at his jaw. "Ain't you got no idea what the man who done the killing looks like so's you can tell I ain't him?"

"Some," Rye replied, and let it hang.

He was beginning to wonder if Dave Pearly could be the murderer. The man in no way matched the description that Jubal Hicks had provided — even if wearing an ankle length duster and with a hat pulled low, and masked, Dave Pearly would not fit. But again, he must take nothing at surface value — and it was best he remember that Hicks was badly hurt at the time, and senses flagging — what he saw might not have registered correctly.

"That mean I look like him?" Pearly

asked, eyes on the bandage encircling Rye's arm.

The lawman was silent briefly. Then, "Maybe."

"Maybe," Pearly repeated in a falling voice. "What's that mean?"

"Folks make mistakes sometimes when they're excited and all worked up. They don't always see things the way they are. I'm more interested in your proving to me that you were in Laramie — and why."

Pearly nodded, wheeled about. "All right, I'll see if I can find the letter. Come on in."

Rye followed the man into the house, passing through a small, overfurnished room that undoubtedly was the parlor, and down a hallway to a second area that Dave Pearly used as an office.

"The wife ain't home," he said, explaining the quiet emptiness of the house. "She's gone to one of them Ladies' Aid meetings — over at the church. Was she here she could probably help me dig up some more of the proof you're wanting."

As the man sat down to a table that served as a desk, Rye glanced about.

There was a calendar on one wall, a large picture of several individuals standing at the entrance to a mine on another, while a third was graced by an oval-framed portrait of a serious-faced woman with an odd shade of blue eyes.

"Yeh, here it is!" Pearly announced suddenly, coming about on the chair, an envelope in his hand. Opening it hastily, he unfolded the sheet and passed it triumphantly to the lawman. "Can see for yourself!"

Rye, features expressionless, noted the date at the top of the letter as well as its contents. Returning it to Pearly, he said, "Backs up what you told me about why you were there — now, can you remember what day it was when you left?"

The man fingered the undertaker's letter thoughtfully. "Well, was a Wednesday when I got to Laramie. We buried Tom that same day — sure — I pulled out early next morning. It would've been Thursday."

Brite had been killed Thursday — sometime during the midmorning hours. Dave Pearly could not have been the killer; not only did nothing tally, but even the time was wrong. Of course, Pearly could be lying about when he rode out of Laramie — but that didn't alter the fact that he came nowhere close to Jubal Hicks' description of the murderer.

"You satisfied now that I didn't kill that there judge you're talking about? If you ain't, and you want some more proof, I expect I can get it up in Laramie. Plenty of local people around, too, that'll stand up for me.

"Been living here for ten years. Retired. Had myself a mine — silver — over on the other side of Leadville. Made myself a pile and then sold out to some New York fellows, and me and my wife settled here. Folks'll tell you I ain't the kind that'd kill a man — and I sure wouldn't have no reason to kill that there judge. Hell's bells, I ain't ever heard of him before now! Where was it you said it happened?"

"Town of Gellen — in Wyoming."

"Gellen?" Pearly repeated, scratching at his chin. "Can't say that I ever heard of it, either, but then I ain't been up to Wyoming more'n a couple or three times. You want me to go with you over to the marshal here? He'll back up all

I've told you — and them folks that claims it was me on the Trail, are they handy? I'll be right glad to go have a talk with them."

"Won't be necessary," Rye said, a heaviness settling within him. He'd been on the wrong track all the time. "I'm obliged to you."

"Was all right, all right!" Pearly said, leading the lawman back to the front porch. "You was only doing what you get paid for."

Rye started to turn away, hesitated. "Did you hear or see anybody on your way down from Laramie?"

Pearly immediately said, "Nope, sure didn't. And there ain't a lot of folks using the old Arapaho nowadays, Marshal, so if there'd been somebody ahead of me, I expect I'd've known it. Goes for being behind me, too."

"I see," the lawman said, starting again for his horse. "Thanks again."

"You're sure more'n welcome, Marshal. Now, if there's anything else you're needing — information, things like that — I'll be right here."

Rye smiled briefly, swung up onto his saddle, and returned to the entrance of the yard. Letting himself out and again securing the gate, he headed back slowly for Billy Grindle's livery barn, his weather-browned face in deep study.

Obviously the rider the Chases had heard was Dave Pearly — and he'd been wrong to assume that it was Brite's murderer. What then had become of the man? Pearly was certain there was no one either behind or in front of him, yet witnesses had observed the killer riding onto the Arapaho Trail and had not seen him double back.

And once in the canyon, as Rye recalled being told and had seen for himself, there were no places where a man could climb out because of the steep, rugged nature of the slopes — with the exception of the one where he'd encountered Red and his two friends, Gabe and Charlie. They evidently knew a way to come in from the mesa above, and had departed by the same route.

But that point, he recalled, was not far from where the canyon ended and the plain that led to the settlement began. A man on the run and forced to remain in the canyon for all that distance, logically, would not choose to climb out at that point since by then he'd not be far from his goal. He'd simply stick to the easier traveling course and hurry on to the crossroad at Alamo Butte.

An idea came into John Rye's mind — a ridiculous thought that made no sense, yet it began to build and take shape regardless of its utter impossibility. And it would not go away.

Abruptly the lawman rocked forward and roweled the chestnut into a lope. Only Patience Chase could give him the answer to what he was thinking.

Twenty

Almost at Grindle's stables, John Rye slowed. Two horses were standing at the rear of the building. Both looked vaguely familiar, and he was certain they had not been there when he rode out for Pearly's place.

Holding the chestnut to a walk, the lawman drew near the livery barn, his narrowed glance now probing restlessly while tiny flags of intuitive warning waved furiously in his mind. Two horses . . . In that moment he recalled Billy Grindle's reply to a question he had asked: *Was a couple of riders showed up here this morning.*

Red and Charlie. It could only be they, and spotting him from somewhere along

217

the street, probably as he rode out to talk with Dave Pearly, they had gone on to the stable and were waiting for him.

Tension now gripping him, turning him sharp and deliberate, the lawman continued on his course down the center of the dusty road. Almost abreast of Grindle's, he veered toward the building, drew up close to the wide doors, and slipped quietly from the saddle. Heading the big horse into the opening, he slapped the animal on the rump and sent him trotting down the runway.

Pistol drawn, cool, Rye waited. There was no reaction from the gloomy depths of the squat building, no sound except the measured, hollow thud of the chestnut's hoofs as, now walking, he proceeded along the hardpack.

Red and Charlie had not taken the bait he offered. Rye, a grim, half smile on his lips, eased nearer to the doorway. He remained there for a long minute considering the advisability of circling the building and entering from the rear; he discarded the idea. It would make no difference — they would be expecting him to try, be all set for him there, too.

He wondered about Patience and Ben

Chase. What had happened to them? Were the outlaws holding them, and perhaps Billy Grindle, hostage? There was a strong possibility of it — assuming that Red and Charlie were actually there, as he suspected. If he was right, and the Chases and Grindle were prisoners, he hoped they'd not harm the woman in any way — and, of course, the same went for the two men. He didn't like the thought of others getting hurt because of him.

Suddenly, deciding to let matters go no further, he ducked low, and closing his eyes briefly to speed their adjustment from the bright sunlight of the street to the dimness within the stables, he plunged through the doorway.

Gunshots instantly shattered the silence in the stable, the blasts setting up a chain of echoes and startling several horses in the rear of the structure into shying and milling nervously about in their stalls. Rye heard bullets thunk into the plank wall behind him as he threw himself from side to side while frantically trying to locate the positions of the two outlaws.

He came up hard against the unyielding end of a stall with his injured arm, recoiled, cursing deeply as pain raced through him. But the thick partition of the stall offered immediate sanctuary from the bullets snapping at him, and he lurched into it, still unable to tell where Red and Charlie were hiding.

Hat off, arm now feeling wet and throbbing persistently, the lawman moved back along the heavy planks to the runway, a hard grin cracking his lips. He reckoned he could stop wondering about it now — the outlaws for sure were there, and waiting for him. Pausing at the corner, upright, Rye sucked in a deep breath, allowed his heaving lungs to recover. The barn was filled with layers of drifting powder smoke, merged with the dust stirred up by the frightened horses in the rear of the structure.

Careful, the lawman peered around the end of the partition separating the stall in which he crouched from the one next in the row, and strained to locate the two outlaws. They had to be somewhere in the back of the building, he knew, since the bullets had come at him from that direction.

Suddenly Patience Chase cried out in

pain. The lawman jerked erect behind the thick planks, anger surging through him.

"You heard that, Marshal?" It was Red's voice.

"I hear," he replied, and quickly moved to the opposite end of the stall. There, standing straight, he looked over the tops of the partitions.

"We got your lady friend here. Figured you'd like to come get her."

Striving to place the sound of the outlaw's voice, or detect a bit of motion, Rye took his time replying. Then, "She's not my lady friend. She and her husband were a couple of pilgrims that I met on the Trail."

"Yeh, sure. How about it — you coming?"

It seemed to the lawman that Red's words were originating in a room at the lower end of the runway. He could see the dark rectangle of an open doorway — probably a place where Billy Grindle stored gear or maybe sacks of grain. Would Charlie be in there, also? It was doubtful. Likely he had taken a position somewhere opposite so that they could trap him in a cross fire.

221

"I ain't hearing you, Marshal —"

Rye forced a laugh, hoping to keep the conversation alive. "Hell, Red, you know I'm not fool enough to do that!"

There was a pause, broken finally when the outlaw said: "I see you got who I am all figured out. Means you know who you're dealing with."

"Yeh — what happened to Charlie?"

"I'm right here!" the second outlaw declared immediately. "Can say I'm the other half of your welcoming committee."

Rye spotted Charlie at that moment. The outlaw had moved, only slightly, but enough to show the lawman where he was standing — behind some bales of hay at the end of the runway, but opposite the room where Red was holed up. Satisfaction now running strong through him, Rye turned his attention back to Red. He must be certain about him.

"Where's the lady's husband?" he called. "You got him there in that tack room, too?"

It was a question with a dual purpose, designed to determine if Ben Chase was with his wife or somewhere outside the stable and could possibly put in an appearance shortly, and if it actually was the room at the end of the runway where Red was making his stand.

"Yeh, he's setting right here with her. Ain't sure if he'll yell or not when I pinch him like I done her, but I can find out."

It definitely was the tack room. Like as not Red had Billy Grindle in there, also, but Rye needed to determine that for certain, too. Grindle could be bringing help, and if so, it would be foolish to rush things.

"Better turn them loose, Red — the stableman, too."

"Naw, he's staying right here with them. Truth is, he couldn't go nowheres right now if he wanted to. Had to lay my gun barrel across his head to make him mind. He's still out — colder'n a dead fish. . . . Now, what about it? You coming after your friends?"

Rye let that ride for a few moments, then, "I can't do that, Red. It'd be a fool stunt. I've got a better idea. They've got nothing to do with you and me, so let's leave them out of it. I'll count to three and then we'll both step out into the runway — it'll be you and Charlie against me. Odds will be in your favor — and that ought to suit you.''

It was Red's turn to laugh. ''Hell, I ain't dumb either, Marshal! You'd let Charlie and me show ourselves and you'd cut us down before we would get a look at you. Nope, you ain't suckering me into that kind of a deal.''

Rye rubbed at his jaw. He had to find a way by which he could get Red out of the tack room, away from his hostages. He now had both outlaws located, could move in fast, take care of Charlie and then open up on Red. But with the others in the probably small area of the room, the risk of them getting hurt was too great. Somehow he must draw the outlaw out — at least into the doorway.

''You coming, Marshal?'' It was Charlie this time.

Rye heaved a loud sigh. ''Guess I ain't got a choice. Sure can't let those folks get hurt. Just have to take my chances —''

''No, Marshal — John — don't!'' Patience broke in, her voice high, hysterical. She was near the breaking point, the lawman suspected.

''Yeh, you're sure right — you ain't got no chance,'' Red said in a tone of

224

satisfaction. "Just you step out there into the middle of the runway and start walking this way."

"Now you're wanting me to be a sucker," Rye said with a scornful laugh. "I'll come down the runway, all right, but it'll be my way — and not out in the middle where you can pot me easy."

"Won't make no difference," Red said, "you're headed for the boneyard any way you at it. . . . Like to ask you something first, before we get at it. Did you shoot Gabe?"

"Sure did. He's laying back up along the Trail — if the buzzards and the coyotes haven't already carried him off."

"Sort of figured you did. Expect you know you plugged me — got me in the leg."

"Yeh, I know."

"Tots up to a couple more things I owe you for, shooting Gabe and putting a bullet into me."

"There something else?"

"Sure is — my brother Earl — Earl Fontana. Was you that brought him in so's that damned judge could string him up."

Earl Fontana . . . The name was

vaguely familiar. "That what this is all about — you wanting to get even with me? Must've been a long time ago," Rye said, and quickly returned to the opposite end of the stall, at the runway.

"Been too damn long!" Red snapped, his manner changing perceptibly. "Been waiting all this time for a chance to square things for Earl. Seen it had come that day you rode out of Gellen, chasing that killer. . . . But I ain't doing no more talking! You coming or you want me to put a slug in one of your friends here as a starter?"

"I'm coming!" Rye shouted, and whipping off his hat threw it at the doorway of the tack room. In that same instant he launched himself full length into the center of the runway.

His first bullet went into Charlie. The outlaw rocked forward, his body stiffening in the dim light. But Rye was giving him no more thought, was already changing position and trying to get in line with the tack room's entrance.

In that fraction of time a yell went up from its shadow-filled depths. Abruptly Red came stumbling through the doorway with Ben Chase close behind.

Rye realized immediately what had taken place. When the outlaw had moved to the room's entrance to watch and wait, the big homesteader had taken matters into his own hands and, rushing forward, shoved Red into the open.

"He's all yours, Mar —"

The blast of Red Fontana's weapon cut off the rest of what Chase intended to say. As Ben rocked back against the wall from the sledging impact of the heavy-caliber bullet at such close range, Rye bounded to his feet to face the outlaw, the screams of Patience blending with the echoes of the gunshot.

Red, too, was pivoting, coming about. The lawman triggered his pistol, felt the scorch of the bullet fired simultaneously by the outlaw as it burned a path across his thigh. He got off another shot, unable to see through the churning smoke and dust if Red was finished and going down or not, but knowing he had to be sure. His second bullet was unnecessary; Fontana was dead.

Tension still holding him in its tight grip, the lawman straightened slowly. Patience burst suddenly through the doorway of the tack room, flung a glance at him, and knelt beside her husband. After a few moments she turned, looked up at the marshal.

"He wants to talk — tell you something."

Rye's tense, rigid silhouette relented. He glanced to the stable's wide entrance where a lone figure, evidently a passerby who had heard the last gunshots, had paused and was looking in, and then moving to where the homesteader lay, crouched beside the woman.

"Sorry how this turned out," Rye said, laying his hand on that of Chase. "Took a lot of guts to do what you did, and I want to thank you —"

"Ain't — no need," Ben said, with a feeble gesture. "I owed you — a'plenty for — what you done — for Patience. Want — want to ask — a favor."

"Name it," the lawman said hurriedly. Ben Chase was dying fast.

"Patience — asking you to see — she get — to them folks — in Texas."

"Can depend on it," Rye assured him. "I'll put her on the stagecoach myself. Would take her there only I'll have to stay here, start looking for that killer. Don't worry none about your wife —"

"Marshal — she ain't my — wife. My sister. And something — else. You can — quit hunting for — that killer. Was me — that shot — Brite."

A tremor of surprise shook the lawman. He stared at the homesteader, shook his arm gently.

"Why?" he asked, bending low to catch Chase's answer. "Why did you kill him?"

There was no reply. Ben Chase was dead.

Twenty One

—John Rye pulled back, got to his feet as Patience began to sob quietly over Chase. That there was a possibility the homesteader was the killer he was searching for had occurred to the lawman shortly after he had talked with Dave Pearly, but it had been a fleeting, farfetched thought, and one he had intended to pursue with great care.

But it was all over now; the hunt for Orson Brite's murderer was finished, having come to a surprising conclusion, and, along with it, another startling revelation; Patience was not married, as he'd been led to believe. A hard grin pulled at the corners of the lawman's mouth. He'd been played for a fool from the night when he'd first met the Chases.

The bystander at the entrance to the stable had ventured nearer, and as Rye came about to face him, he said: "There some kind of trouble here?"

With the lifeless bodies of both outlaws and Ben Chase clearly in view, the question was ludicrous. But Rye was in no mood for humor, however unintentional.

"Go get the marshal," he directed.

"Yes, sir," the bystander said, and, wheeling, retreated hurriedly to the street.

There was a scuffing in the doorway of the tack room, and Billy Grindle, staggering slightly and rubbing the back of his head gingerly, came out into the runway. He halted, glanced around, finally focused his eyes on Rye.

"You got them, I see," he said, pointing at Red Fontana and Charlie, last name still unknown to them.

The lawman shrugged, looked down at Ben Chase and Patience. Grindle moved a few steps closer.

"Him, too? How'd it happen? Last I seen of him he was setting there alongside the lady. I recollect starting to get up and then that redheaded one hit me and all the lights went out."

"It was him that shoved Fontana out to where I could get a shot. Cost him his life."

Grindle wagged his head dolefully. "Was a mighty fine fellow — and it sure is a shame. I'm sorry, missus. It was a brave thing he done."

Rye stepped up close to the woman and, taking her by the shoulders, brought her upright. Holding her in his arms, he nodded to Grindle.

"I'll be obliged if you'll look after him," he said. "The lady'll probably want to bury him tomorrow."

The stable owner nodded. "Sure," and turned to the doorway. A half-a-dozen men, one wearing a star, had entered, were hurrying up.

"It's the marshal, Artie Flynn," Grindle said. "Surprises me some him a'hearing the shots —"

"I sent for him," Rye explained as the elderly lawman halted nearby. Reaching into a pocket, the federal marshal drew out his identification and displayed it to Flynn, who read quickly and nodded.

"One with the red hair is named

Fontana," Rye said then, returning the leather fold to its place. "Other one is Charlie somebody. Both outlaws. Expect you've got wanted dodgers on both of them. You need any more details on what happened Grindle there can supply them. If you want me, I'll be at the hotel — if you've got one here."

"We have — right on down the street. The doctor's right next door to it, so you can get that arm fixed up, too," Flynn said, and pointed at Ben. "Who's he?"

"This lady's brother. He was being held hostage by those two, along with her and Grindle so's they could get at me. Was him that helped me bring them down. I owe him plenty."

"I see. You ain't said yet what his name is."

"Ben Chase. He's from —"

"No," Patience broke in, "his name's not Chase, it's Canady — Ben Canady."

Patience was sitting on the edge of the bed in the hotel room when Rye, carrying two cups and a small pot of coffee, returned after a brief absence. She had bathed her face and neck, combed her hair, and, in general,

233

straightened up her clothing, he saw, and looked to be in much better spirits.

Placing the tray on a table, the lawman first raised the room's solitary window to relieve the trapped, warm air, and then filling each cup from the pot of steaming, black liquid, he passed one to her and settled back in a chair with the other.

"It's been a bad time for you, but —" he began, and stopped short when Patience checked his words.

"Before this goes a moment longer I want to tell you how ashamed I am that we deceived you —"

A wry grin pulled at the lawman's lips. The realization that he'd been taken in had angered him considerably when it first came to light. But that had passed and now he was merely curious as to why it had been necessary.

"Forget it. Was about to say they've got a telegraph office here. Can have them send my report in, save myself some writing. First need to clear up a couple of things, however."

"I'm all right," the woman said, her relief apparent. "What do you need to know?"

"What Ben said about being the one

who killed Brite — is that true?"

"Yes, it is."

"You know why he did?"

Patience stared into her cup as if mustering the necessary words, while outside in the street a rider went by at a fast gallop, stirring up a chorus of protest from a half-a-dozen or so excited dogs.

"To start with," she said finally, "my pa was Rufus Canady. Does that mean anything to you?"

Rye gave it thought, found it struck no chord in his mind. "No, sure doesn't."

"Well, we lived on a homestead up in Montana, just like we said. But after Ma died Pa got sort of restless and every now and then he would up and disappear. He'd be gone sometimes for a month — even longer. He always came back, though — except for one time.

"We got worried and Ben started asking around about him. He found out from the sheriff in town near where we lived that Pa was being held for murder at a place called Gellen — over in Wyoming."

"And the judge was Orson Brite —"

"Yes . . . Ben and I went over there as soon as we could get some folks to look after the place and our livestock. We got there the day before the trial started."

Patience hesitated for a sip of coffee and then continued. "Pa swore to us that he was innocent, and to us it looked like he had proof that he was, all right. But the judge barely listened to it and sentenced Pa and the man who'd been with him to hang.

"Ben lost his head when the judge pronounced the sentence and jumped up and went after him. He jerked Brite out of his chair and knocked him down, all the time yelling that Pa wasn't a murderer and that he wasn't getting a fair trial.

"It ended up with the judge having Ben arrested and then tried, and sentenced him to the penitentiary for five years — right then and there. I stayed around until they took Pa away to be hung and Ben off to the pen, and then I went back home to figure out what was I going to do."

Patience sighed, stared out through the streaky glass of the window at the rolling land beyond the settlement, all light and shadow now in the late afternoon hour.

"I guess I'm in the same fix again — I don't know what to do next."

"We'll talk about that later," Rye said. He guessed he had the complete story of the Canady family figured out in his head, but reckoned it was best if he heard it from Patience.

"Did you go to see Ben while he was in the pen?"

She nodded. "It was a year before I found out where he was. He sent me a letter and I made the trip right away. He just wanted to tell me to stay there on the farm, that he'd come home as soon as his sentence was up. He was terribly bitter and I had a feeling that this Judge Brite had not seen the last of him.

"But I did like he said. I was only sixteen then so you can see I didn't have much choice. The folks who had come to look after our place had stayed on, so I lived with them — or they with me, whichever you want to say.

"Time went by and then one day I was out in the yard. I heard a horse coming up the road and looked up. It was Ben. He was so much older and thinner, but he said he was all right, and that we were moving to Texas. He'd had all of

Montana and Wyoming he wanted.

"We spent the next couple of weeks getting ready, and then rode out. We'd sold our livestock for whatever we could get for it, and just turned the place over to the couple I told you about — the ones who'd been living there with me. What we had wasn't worth much, anyway."

"When did Ben go to Gellen — where the judge was?" Rye asked.

"I didn't know anything about that until it was all over. We traveled over into Wyoming — Ben said he wanted to see a man in Laramie that he'd met in the pen who could tell him the best way to Texas. We went there and then rode on toward the Colorado line where we were going to follow this trail Ben's friend told him about."

"The Arapaho Trail," Rye supplied.

"Yes. When we got almost to Colorado, Ben said he'd have to go back, that he needed to buy a gun. We'd have to have one, but he'd just forgot. We made a sort of camp in the trees and then he told me to wait there, that he'd only be gone a couple of hours.

"I was tired from riding so I didn't argue with him about it. He was back in closer to four hours than two, and we packed up and moved right on — and kept going until long after dark.

"We stopped then and made a decent camp and spent the rest of the night. I remember Ben was real quiet and had very little to say about anything, but I just figured he was tired. I remember hearing that rider, too, that he mentioned. It was the man you went to see after we got here."

The lawman nodded, drained the last of the coffee from his cup. "Had a talk with him. . . . Did Ben ever tell you that he'd killed Judge Brite?"

"Not for a while — was only after you showed up, in fact. He told you that I was his wife, and I couldn't understand why. Then a little later he gave me the whole story — of how he'd doubled back to Gellen, after telling me he had to go get a gun, and shot Brite for what he'd done to Pa and him — and me — and then rode off. He'd stopped along the way and buried the clothes he'd been wearing — that long coat and the old hat and that bandanna he'd used for a mask."

Patience paused, faced Rye squarely.

"I want to tell you again that I'm sorry we misled you. I guess, when we found out you were a lawman I should have told you the truth — but Ben was my brother and I couldn't bring myself around to doing it."

"Not hard to understand," Rye said, refilling her cup as well as his own with coffee. It was now cold and not particularly appetizing.

"Will — will I go to jail for not being honest with you — for being a part of it?"

The marshal shrugged. "Not far as I'm concerned. Appears to me you were sort of caught in the middle and had to go along with your brother in it. A judge like Orson Brite might not agree with me — but that's how I see it."

"Thank you, John," Patience said softly, using his given name once again. "I'll always be grateful, and" — she hesitated, a wistfulness coming into her eyes — "and hopeful."

He shook his head. "Something we can both do — hope."

Patience sighed deeply, studied his hard-set, inscrutable features for a long minute. And then, as if saying farewell to her dreams of a future with him, once and for all time, she smiled sadly and shrugged.

"Where will you go now?"

"Texas," he said unexpectedly. "I told a fine man I knew that I'd put his sister on a stagecoach for there, but I've changed my mind. The lady and I've both got a bit of business to tend to tomorrow, and soon as it's done, I'm taking her there personally."

Patience was smiling again, this time happily. "I'll be ready when you are, Marshal," she said.

A note on the text
Large print edition designed by
Bernadette Montalvo
Composed in 16 pt Times Roman
on a Mergenthaler Linotron 202
by Modern Graphics, Inc.

X

K

S

L

B